A Note to Readers

While Mark and Holly and their friends and family are fictional, their story is based on real events. During the early 1900s, families were being exposed to more music because of the gramophone. No longer did they have to rely on local concerts or on music that they made themselves in their parlors.

Marching bands were extremely popular, and almost every town had a bandstand in one of its parks. The local band would give concerts in the park every week during the summer.

John Philip Sousa was one of the most popular musicians of his day. He performed throughout the country and the world, including appearances in Minneapolis. The words Mr. Sousa speaks about music in this book are taken from his writings.

Mr. Sousa's marches are still played by school bands and professional orchestras. Fourth of July fireworks wouldn't seem complete without hearing his "Stars and Stripes Forever" with its famous piccolo solo.

MARCHING

with

SOUSA

Norma Jean Lutz

PUBLISHING, INC.
Uhrichsville, Ohio

To Lloyd and Frances Kidwell.
Thanks for all the love you poured into my daughter!

© MCMXCVIII by Barbour Publishing, Inc.

ISBN 1-57748-406-1

Published by Barbour Publishing, Inc.
P.O. Box 719
Uhrichsville, Ohio 44683
http://www.barbourbooks.com

ecpa Member of the
Evangelical Christian
Publishers Association

Printed in the United States of America.

Cover illustration by Peter Pagano.
Inside illustrations by Adam Wallenta.

CHAPTER 1

Summer Brass Band

Mark Morgan stared at the sheet music on the stand in front of him in a vain attempt to concentrate. The band room was stuffy and crowded, and the students restless. The windows were open, but Mark was on the far side of the room away from the cool May breeze that periodically blew in.

Mr. Schoggen, the band director, tapped the music stand with his wooden baton to bring the students to order. They'd been practicing the numbers they were to play at the Fair Oaks Elementary School commencement exercises. One part of the Sousa march "The Thunderer" was giving them problems.

"Come now, class," Mr. Schoggen said. "One would think the members of my band had spring fever. Once again from the top."

Mark pressed the cool metal mouthpiece of his trumpet to his lips and focused on the powerful piece. The arrangement was pure Sousa genius, and this section was Mark's favorite part—the finale where the trumpets led out with vibrant energy.

He'd worked on this piece only a short while before his trip to San Francisco with his family. And of course there'd been no opportunities to practice his trumpet while traveling. Now commencement exercises were only three weeks away—not much time to get it down pat.

Mr. Schoggen's eyes were half-closed as he waved the baton in rhythmic sweeps, pulling the band members together as one harmonic unit. His head tipped back just a little, as he leaned first to one side, then to the other in time with the tempo.

Suddenly, his eyes flew open and the baton came down hard on the music stand. All instruments shrieked to a stop. "Jens Kubek! Harvey Newmire!" Mr. Schoggen exclaimed. "What's the meaning of this?"

Mark glanced in the direction of his good friend Jens. Jens and Harvey sat side by side in the clarinet section. They'd been fooling around nearly all band hour, snickering and jabbing at one another. Mark wondered what Jens could possibly be thinking. Mark and Jens both loved Mr. Schoggen's class, so why was Jens acting so silly? And with Harvey Newmire of all people.

Mr. Schoggen gave the boys a stern warning and once more raised his baton. "Very well, students," he said, "take it from the top."

Now it was even more difficult for Mark to concentrate. Focus. That was one of Mr. Schoggen's favorite words. Focus on the music, the rhythm, the expression. Focus on what the composer is saying. All Mark could think of was Jens and Harvey acting silly together. Before Mark had left for San Francisco, Harvey was the last person Jens would ever have buddied up with.

Trumpet to his lips. Focus on the deep breathing. The finale approached. Mr. Schoggen's eyes popped open as Mark didn't quite reach the high notes. Mr. Schoggen's free hand was palm up as though he were pushing, pushing the notes upward. Mark sat up straighter, breathed deeper and came up under the notes just as he'd been taught.

The crescendo of the piece filled the room and pressed into all corners. Reverberations from the bass drum echoed in Mark's midsection. He could feel the pounding to the soles of his feet. Cymbals crashed, the snare drum rolled. Mr. Schoggen's face grew redder as the final notes came together in exhilarating harmony.

The last flick of the baton cut each note off. "Good, good," Mr. Schoggen said. "Could be better, but it is good. Before you are dismissed. . ." He went to his desk, shuffled through papers, found what he was looking for, and returned to the group.

"I've been given an announcement," he said, looking at them over his glasses. "Mr. Klawinski, conductor of the Minneapolis Brass Band, will begin a program this summer allowing junior members to audition."

Mark caught Jens's attention and smiled. Junior members of the brass band! What an opportunity!

"This includes seventh- and eighth-grade students only," Mr. Schoggen continued. The fifth and sixth graders groaned. "Those who pass the auditions will march in the Fourth of July parade and will play concerts with the band in the bandstand at

Central Park every Sunday afternoon throughout the summer."

Mark's breath caught in his throat. Studying under Mr. Klawinski would be a chance of a lifetime.

Jens's hand shot up. When Mr. Schoggen acknowledged him, he asked, "What about uniforms? Will the junior members wear uniforms?"

Mark and Jens had always admired the band members' smart-looking uniforms, complete with military hats, gold braid, and brass buttons.

Mr. Schoggen scanned further down the page. "Uniforms are provided," he said, "but must be returned at the end of the summer."

Mark smiled at Jens, and they both nodded. In his mind's eye, Mark could see them stepping out in cadence at the July Fourth parade, probably playing a rousing Sousa march, with all the city of Minneapolis on hand to watch. A shiver crawled up Mark's back at the thought.

"Where are the auditions held?" another student asked.

"Above Rose Drugstore," Mr. Schoggen answered, "which is where the brass band rehearses. We'll know more about scheduling later." Pulling out his pocket watch, he announced that class was dismissed.

Mark pulled the mouthpiece from his trumpet and laid it and the horn in his black leather case. He'd have to practice with a vengeance during the next few weeks or he'd never make it into the brass band for the summer.

"Mark, did you hear that?" Jens was beside him, his clarinet already packed away in his case. "The brass band!"

"I heard it. I still can't believe it, but I heard it."

"Remember how we admired those uniforms last summer?"

"And the summer before that," Mark reminded him.

Jens laughed. "And now *we* have a chance to wear one."

Harvey came up behind Jens just then. "And we're all eligible to try out," he added.

Mark didn't want to be impolite, but no one had invited Harvey Newmire into this conversation. Jens gave Harvey a friendly punch in the arm. "You got nothing to worry about, Harvey. You're the best clarinetist here. You'll have no trouble making it."

Mark didn't think Harvey was all that good. In fact, what Harvey did best was get into trouble. Miss Ronan had put him in the corner with the dunce cap three times this year. That is, at least three times that Mark knew of. She might have done it again while Mark had been in San Francisco.

"Come on slowpoke," Jens said to Mark, "or Miss Ronan will mark us tardy."

As the three of them went out of the band room, Mr. Schoggen said, "Mark, will you stop and see me before you leave school this afternoon?"

Mark glanced at his instructor to see if he were in trouble, but Mr. Schoggen was smiling. "Yes, sir. Will it take long?"

"Not long."

Out in the hall, Jens said, "What do you suppose he wants?"

Mark shrugged. "Beats me. Will you wait for me?" Mark nearly always walked with Jens to his place before going on home.

"Sure," Jens said, then turned to Harvey. "Can you come over for a while?"

Mark froze. Why would Jens want to invite Harvey to tag along?

But Harvey shook his head. "Naw. Mama said for me to come right home. I think she's got chores for me."

Mark heaved an inward sigh of relief. Back in the seventh-grade classroom, the band students put their instruments on the shelf in the cloakroom then took their seats. Miss Ronan asked them to take out their history books. Boring history was not one of Mark's favorite subjects. Why study about dull past events when so much was happening right now?

Just then, a chugging sound came from the street in front of the school as an automobile rumbled by. Mark gazed out the window at the vehicle, as did every other boy in the classroom. It was Mr. Zuckerman, who owned the dry goods store down the street.

Miss Ronan smiled. "I don't believe that automobile is coming to take anyone in this room for a spin, so let's bring our eyes back inside the classroom please."

Her remark created a twitter among the students. For the most part, the students liked the good-natured Miss Ronan. She'd been especially cooperative when Mark's stepfather, Christopher Wilkins, asked to take Mark out of school for the trip to California. When she learned that Mark had lived through the devastating earthquake in San Francisco, she'd understood why much of his assigned work had not been finished.

"We've been talking about the growth of our United States," she said as she pulled down the map in the front of the room. "Please turn to section seven in your books." Over the rustle of turning pages, she said, "We have a student in our class who has just returned from having experienced a bit of history."

Suddenly all eyes fixed on Mark. His neck and ears felt hot.

Miss Ronan held up the thick history book. "Students, did you realize that the events of the times in which you live will be the history lessons of tomorrow? One day when Mark reads historical accounts of the earthquake, he can say he not only remembers it, but he experienced it."

Stepping away from her desk, she came near to where

Mark was sitting. "Mark," she said, "before the school term is out, I want you to tell this class about California and about the earthquake. I understand from your sister Holly that you have photographs."

Mark wasn't sure what to say. Talking in front of other students wasn't an easy thing for him to do. Looking at Miss Ronan's kind face, he knew it would be difficult to say no.

"By sharing your adventures, you'll help make history come alive for us."

Mark swallowed hard. Perhaps with the photographs in hand he could do it.

"This is not an assignment," Miss Ronan added, "but a request."

Mark gave a slight nod. "Yes, ma'am, I'll try."

Miss Ronan smiled again. "Good. Just let me know when you're ready, and we'll make time during history period."

It was difficult to listen to the rest of the history lesson because Mark's mind went back to the terrible earthquake and the raging fires and explosions that followed. Upon their return, his stepfather, Christopher, had written a number of articles about the event for magazines and newspapers. His byline was showing up all across the nation. Mama said that was God's way of bringing blessing from tragedy.

When school let out, Mark hurried to the cloakroom to grab his lunch pail, his cap, and his instrument case. "Don't forget to wait for me," he said to Jens as they bounded down the stairs.

"I said I'd wait, didn't I?" Jens headed for the wide double doors. "I'll be out by the swings."

Mark stood looking after his friend. Jens's tone had been anything but friendly. Something strange was happening to Jens, and Mark had no idea what it was.

In the band room, Mark learned that Mr. Schoggen only wanted to advise him about his upcoming solo for the commencement exercises.

"I know you were unable to practice for several weeks," Mr. Schoggen said. "I believe you're doing well, but I want you to promise you'll spend at least an hour a day practicing between now and your performance."

"Yes, sir," Mark said. Actually he'd like to practice more than an hour a day. He loved practicing his trumpet. The problem was, the rest of the family didn't always appreciate the "noise," as they called it. "I know I need extra practice."

"Not only for your solo, but also for the brass band audition. You do plan to try out?"

"Yes, sir!"

Mr. Schoggen smiled. His dark eyes shone from behind his thick, dark-rimmed glasses. "I thought so. I see potential in you, Mark. Being a member of that prestigious group will teach you a great deal."

Mark basked in the welcome compliment. "Thank you, sir!"

"One more thing," Mr. Schoggen said as he pulled a piece of paper from his desk. "I knew you and Jens would be interested in this article from *Music* magazine."

Mark took the paper. It was a clipping of an article about Mr. Sousa, and the March King's photograph was at the top. Just wait until Jens saw this one! He and Jens collected articles and photographs of their music hero. "Thank you, sir. Thank you very much," he said.

"You may go now," Mr. Schoggen said. "See you tomorrow."

"See you tomorrow." Mark stuffed the clipping into his arithmetic book and hurried out the door.

Jens was waiting at the swings, but there was no smile on his face.

"Come on, Jens," Mark said in as jovial tone as he could muster. "Let's see if your mama's left any snacks for us."

Still sullen, Jens fell into step with Mark. As they walked out of the schoolyard and down the street, Mark told him what Mr. Schoggen had wanted. "He's onto me to practice harder," Mark said. "But I'll have to try to find a time when Christopher isn't writing, when Allyson isn't studying, when Carol isn't grading papers, and when Holly isn't practicing her piano lessons. Sounds impossible, doesn't it?"

Mark's feeble attempt at humor fell on deaf ears. Trying once more to get his friend to talk, he said, "Sometimes I think our trip to San Francisco caused me more trouble than it was worth."

Jens glared at Mark. "To tell the truth, I'm getting tired of hearing you brag on and on about that trip you took. One would think you're the only person in the world who ever went to California. Who cares about any old earthquake anyway? And now we'll have to be bored stiff while you give a talk about it."

Mark stopped short. Could this be his best friend talking?

CHAPTER 2
Ragtime Music

"Oh, don't look so innocent," Jens went on. "I think you like bragging about all that happened to you."

Mark didn't know what to say. He'd never had to defend himself with Jens before. "That's not true, Jens. Giving a speech wasn't my idea, it was Miss Ronan's."

Just then, he remembered the Sousa article. He pulled it out of his book. "Hey, I almost forgot. Look what Mr. Schoggen gave me. Another article. Here, it's yours. I think I got the last one."

To Mark's delight—and relief—Jens took the paper and began scanning the article. They walked past several blocks of tree-lined streets flanked by rows of two-story houses until they came to the business section where the family butcher shop was located. Across the front of the three-story brick building, printed in large white letters, were the words *Kubek's Butcher Shop*. Jens lived with his family in the rooms above the shop.

Parked at the curb out front was the dray belonging to Jens's father, Fritz Kubek. Jens's older brother, Dirk, was loading meat orders, wrapped neatly in white butcher paper, to deliver to customers. The roan dray horse they called Valdis stood quietly munching oats from the canvas feed bag. The boys both gave the old horse a friendly pat on the side as they went by.

"It's about time you got home," Dirk said to Jens.

Eighteen-year-old Dirk was always rather short with Jens. Mark was grateful his older brother Peter wasn't like that. "It was my fault, Dirk," Mark put in quickly. "I had to talk to the band director, and Jens waited for me."

Dirk didn't even look their way as he took another package from a large basket and transferred it onto the dray. "That explains *this* time," he said, as though Jens were always late from school. Mark knew that wasn't true at all.

"Come on, Mark," Jens said, pulling at Mark's sleeve. "Come up to my room for a while."

"There's no time to dillydally today," Dirk called after them. "Papa needs your help."

Jens didn't answer but led the way into the shop, which was filled with the aromas of all types of meat—from leg of lamb to plucked duck, from fat hams to chopped beef. And, of course, yards and yards of German sausages hung from racks. Jens greeted his parents, who were working behind the counter, and gave his mother a kiss on the cheek.

"You have good day at school, yes?" she asked.

"Fair to middlin'," Jens answered with little enthusiasm. "Is there anything for us to eat?"

"Jens Kubek," Mr. Kubek said sternly, "you will speak to your mama with a tone of respect."

Jens glanced at Mark and gave a shrug. "I had a good day, Mama," he said.

"Don't forget to tell them about the brass band," Mark suggested, trying to be of help.

"What is this about a band?" Mrs. Kubek asked as she scrubbed the cutting boards with hot soapy water. "Already you are in a band."

"We have a chance to audition to play with the Municipal Brass Band for the summer," Jens told her.

"Practice hard and you will make it," his mama said simply—as though her saying it would make it so. Her strong arm moved in circular motions, causing the kerchief that covered her hair to bob up and down in the back. Mrs. Kubek didn't wear her hair piled on top of her head as other women in the city did. Rather she fastened it in a knot at the nape of her neck and kept it covered with a flowered kerchief. Mark often wondered why she dressed as though she still lived in Germany.

"No brass band today," Mr. Kubek's voice boomed out again. "So change from the school clothes and come to help your mama and me."

"Yes, sir," Jens answered. "Come on, Mark."

Mark followed Jens through the store to the stairway in the back room.

"Fresh *Hefekuchen* there is in the bread box," Mrs. Kubek called after them.

Together they took the stairs two at a time. The door at the top of the narrow staircase opened onto the kitchen, which was scrubbed as clean as the shop downstairs. The boys grabbed thick slices of the fresh dark bread, then went through the parlor to the stairwell. On the bureau by the Tiffany lamp was a daguerreotype of Jens's other brother, Kaspar. Kaspar had died of influenza three years ago. That was before the Kubeks had moved to this neighborhood and before Mark ever knew them.

Mark had been told by Jens that Kaspar was a kind, gentle brother. In some ways, it was as though the family still grieved his passing. Mark guessed it was like the way he still thought of Father and wished he could talk to him again. Even though he and his stepfather, Christopher, got along fine, sometimes Father's face and voice would creep into Mark's thoughts just as he was trying to fall asleep at night.

Mark followed Jens up the stairs to the third story, where the family bedrooms were located. Jens's small room faced the back alley, and right outside the window was a metal fire escape. Sometimes on hot summer nights, Jens would take his blankets and sleep out on the landing. His room was simply furnished with a bureau, a wardrobe, a small cot, and a washstand. The wall by the cot was filled with pictures of John Philip Sousa. Mark's bedroom at home was similarly arrayed.

Mark studied the collection for a moment. "Where're you going to put your latest addition?" he said around a mouthful of *Hefekuchen*. "Your walls are almost full."

"I've decided to put this one in my scrapbook," Jens said, pulling a thick bound book from under his bed.

Mark didn't say that the last article they found had also gone to Jens. He didn't bring it up because of the testy mood

Jens had been in ever since Mark's return from California. In light of all that had happened, Mark didn't think it mattered who got which clipping.

"Don't you wish Mr. Sousa would come back to Minneapolis again?" Mark asked, gazing at a photograph of Sousa in his dark uniform complete with the smart military hat and braid trim. They'd attended a Sousa concert at the opera house over a year ago, but their seats were so far up in the balcony, they could hardly see the stage. The music, however, filled the auditorium with all its power and dynamic rhythm.

Mark would never forget the emotions he experienced when every person in the entire place stood to their feet at the opening strains of "Stars and Stripes Forever." It was as though the audience was hypnotized by the rousing music. The two boys talked of nothing but Sousa music for weeks.

"Maybe if he came again, we could get front row seats," Jens said with a grin.

Mark laughed at the joke. As though they would ever have that much money for such a thing. "It's a nice dream," he replied. "What does that article say?" Mark asked sitting down on the cot. "I didn't have a chance to read it."

Together they read the clipping in which the writer proclaimed not only Sousa's composing and conducting genius, but also his showmanship. " 'No other conductor can enthrall an audience as can Sousa,' " Jens read out loud. To Mark he added, "They're not telling us anything we don't know." Reading on, he quoted:

The state legislature in Olympia, Washington, could transact no business on the afternoon of the Sousa matinee because the majority of both houses sat in the concert. A messenger who had

18

*been dispatched to the concert to round up a
quorum ended up staying for the rest of the show
himself.*

Together they laughed at the thought of these important politicians enjoying themselves at a Sousa concert like little boys playing hooky from school.

"Anyway, enough about Sousa." Jens tucked the article in with other bits of papers and mementos in the scrapbook. "Right now, I have something else to show you."

"What is it?"

"You'll see." Returning the scrapbook to its place beneath the bed, he stepped to the wardrobe, opened the doors, and opened a drawer on the bottom. Reaching beneath a layer of clothing, he pulled out a gramophone record.

"So what's so special about a gramophone record?" Mark wanted to know.

Jens handed it over so Mark could see. He read the label. " 'Peacherine Rag.' Jens Kubek, where'd you get this?"

Jens smiled. "Harvey traded it to me for two of my steelies."

"Your best marbles? But you know we're not allowed to listen to ragtime music."

"Hey, don't get all upset. I may trade him back later. There's no harm in listening." Jens turned toward the door. "Come with me. Wait'll you hear what the clarinetist does in this song. It's like nothing you ever heard before!"

Mark hesitated. Not only had Mama warned him against vulgar music, but Mr. Schoggen had also told the band that ragtime amounted to nothing but junk.

"Are you coming or not?"

"Well, I guess one time won't matter." What could it hurt to listen once? Jens had been acting so strangely lately, Mark

19

didn't want to rock the boat.

Down the stairs they tiptoed, snickering as they went. It was not as though anyone were going to hear them. Dirk was making deliveries, and Mr. and Mrs. Kubek were busy with customers. In the parlor, Jens lifted the lid on the gramophone, put the record on, and gave the crank a few turns. When the needle was set in place, Mark was surprised at the music that came out. It was nothing like march rhythm. Nothing like a waltz or a polka.

Jens's face was wreathed in a smile. "What do you think?" he asked.

"I'm not sure," Mark answered as honestly as he could. "It's so different."

Jens snapped his fingers and tapped his toe to the beat. "Great trade, don't you agree? And Harvey has more of these. He tells me that he listens to rags all the time."

"Who's playing the music?"

"They're called the Five Musical Spillers. Harvey says groups like this are playing ragtime in New York City and in New Orleans. All the big important places."

The song lasted for only a few minutes, after which Jens moved the needle and started it up again.

"Don't you think we'd better put it away?" Mark was feeling twinges of guilt. Mama would absolutely faint if she ever found out.

"Just one more time. I want you to listen to the wild clarinet. Listen real close."

Mark leaned closer to the big fluted gramophone horn. He could hear the clarinet all right. It sounded something like a lonely dog in an alley, whimpering and wailing. Then it sounded as though the music has escaped from any proper written notes on a page and run off to play its own way with its very own sound. Mark never knew music could sound like that.

Just then, the door burst open. It was Dirk. "Well, well," he said in that big-brother-knows-it-all tone. "Would you take a look at this."

CHAPTER 3

Mark in Trouble

Dirk strode across the room, lifted the needle, and grabbed the record. "Good thing I had to come upstairs for my hat before I left." He looked at the record label and frowned. "What kind of garbage is this?"

"None of your business," Jens snapped back. "That's mine." He tried to grab it from Dirk's hand, but his older brother moved too quickly. "Give it back," Jens demanded.

"You have money to be spending on garbage?"

"I traded for it, and it's mine." Jens tried again to grab the record. Again, Dirk jerked it away.

"We'll see what Papa has to say about this." With that, Dirk went out the door, slamming it behind him.

"Oh, no," Mark moaned as Dirk's steps pounded down the stairs.

"Don't worry, it's me who's in trouble. And it sure won't be the first time."

But that wasn't exactly true. When Mr. Kubek called them down into the back room, his face was as red as a side of beef. He called them two hooligans who had nothing better to do than listen to evil music. Behind him stood Jens's mama, tsking through her teeth and shaking her head. "If only you could be more like Kaspar," she said softly. "Kaspar would never do such a thing to upset Papa so."

"Now young man," Mr. Kubek continued with Jens, "to your room you will go. I be there in a moment to give you a sound spanking." Turning to Mark, he said, "As for you, I shall use the telephone to tell your mama the trouble you have made."

"But Papa," Jens started, but Mr. Kubek pointed to the door. Jens had to leave.

Mark did not stay to hear what Mr. Kubek said on the telephone to Mama, but he could imagine how it sounded. Mark wondered if Jens would get the record back. As mad as Mr. Kubek was, he'd probably break it into a hundred pieces and toss it all in the ash can in the alley.

As Mark walked down Vine Place to his house, his steps slowed. His trumpet case and schoolbooks felt like lead. How he dreaded facing Mama. Ever since Father died, he tried hard to help Mama and be as good as he could be, never causing any trouble.

In the leafy trees above his head, the noisy jays and mockingbirds fussed. A fat robin hopped down the sidewalk just a few feet ahead. The bird stopped momentarily. It cocked his head as though to ask Mark what could be wrong on such a glorious day.

As he stepped up on the wide front porch of their two-story house, Mark stopped and thought. Perhaps it would be best to go in through the kitchen. Besides, Stella would probably have a snack for him.

Running around the house, he stepped onto the sunporch and went down the hall. Sounds of Holly practicing her piano lessons in the front parlor drifted throughout the house. As he pushed open the swinging door into the kitchen, there stood Mama and Stella at the stove. Mark stopped dead in his tracks.

"Hello, Mama. Stella." He hurried to Mama's side and gave her a kiss. "I know Mr. Kubek called you," he said quickly, "but it's not like what you think."

Mama glanced over at Stella, then looked back at Mark. "Perhaps you should come into the back parlor and talk about it. Take your things to your room first. Stella, bring a snack for Mark, would you please?"

"Of course, Mrs. Morgan. Sorry," she said all flustered at her verbal blunder. "I meant to say Mrs. Wilkins."

Mama smiled. "I know, Stella. It's all right. I'm still getting used to the new name myself."

Presently, Mark was munching on oatmeal cookies as he and Mama sat together in the back parlor. He did his best to explain exactly what happened. But he left out the part of how strangely Jens had been acting. Maybe that had been his imagination. He just wasn't sure.

Mama listened quietly. Then she said, "I agree with Mr. Kubek that such music is dangerous. Such jazzed-up sounds can only come to no good. The Lord wants us to listen to good music just as He would want us to read good literature." Mama sat straight in her wing-backed chair. "We must choose between good and bad in many things in this world," she continued.

24

"You should have the strength and wherewithal to choose the good each time."

Mark wanted to tell her that the music wasn't really bad. Mama had probably never heard ragtime music before. But he knew better than to interrupt.

At one point he started to ask if she were going to tell Christopher, but thought better of it. If she were going to tell him, Christopher would have been with them during this conversation.

At supper that evening, Mark didn't talk much. With three girls—four, counting Mama—a fellow didn't have much chance to squeeze a word in. Since Allyson was studying at Normal School to be a teacher and since Carol was a fifth grade teacher at Washington Elementary, they talked on and on about school. It made Mark feel like he could never escape school.

As Stella served the roast and vegetables, Carol told about her problems with a difficult boy in her class. Allyson asked questions on how the problems were handled. Then she quipped, "I hope I never have a boy in my class quite so contrary as that."

"Every class has at least one student who seems to cause problems constantly," Carol told her. Mark thought of Harvey.

Then Holly broke in to tell the family that her teacher had asked her to give a talk on their trip to California and the earthquake.

"You, too?" Mark asked. "Miss Ronan asked me the same thing."

Carol laughed. "It sounds as though your teachers have been talking to one another."

"May we take our photographs to school, Mama?" Holly asked.

Mama nodded. "I see no reason why not. What do you think, Christopher?"

Christopher, who had been quietly listening and enjoying his supper, nodded. "By all means. That's what's so wonderful about photographs. It allows you to share your experiences with others. That's why my editors ask me to take photographs as well as write articles."

Mark wasn't nearly as excited about this project as Holly was. He could tell by the expression on her face that she was delighted at the thought of standing in front of her fifth grade class and sharing every little detail. Mark was not at all delighted. And if it were going to make Jens any more unhappy, he'd like to skip it altogether.

"What Miss Ronan ought to do," Mark suggested, "is join our class with yours and have you talk to both grades."

"You're missing the whole point," Carol told him. "Your teacher not only wants the class to learn about your trip, but she also wants you to gain confidence in your ability to address the group."

"I'm sure that's true, Mark," Mama agreed.

Mark tried not to groan. Surely the hours of recitation he'd done in years past had taken care of that.

"Mark," Carol said, "I expected by now to hear all about your trying out for the Municipal Brass Band. The information came to our school today."

With everything that had happened at Jens's house, Mark had quite forgotten his exciting news.

"What's this all about?" Allyson wanted to know. "Mark's to be in the brass band? *The* brass band?"

"Only if I make the auditions," Mark put in, feeling a little embarrassed about the whole thing. After all, he might not make it. The competition would be stiff.

"Tell us the details," Mama said, leaning out of the way so Stella could refill her water glass.

"Carol can tell about it," he answered, deferring to his older sister.

"Mr. Victor Klawinski has decided to allow junior band members to join up with the band for the summer," Carol explained. "He's asked for those who are interested to audition. But only seventh and eighth graders."

"I've met Mr. Klawinski," Christopher put in. "I interviewed him when he first took over the band a few years ago. Nice fellow. Very talented."

"Since our band at Washington School started only last year," Carol went on, "we have no students who are qualified."

"When are the auditions, Mark?" This from Allyson.

Carol answered for him. "The week before commencement."

"That's not far off," Holly said. "Are you nervous? Will you wear a uniform and play concerts with the band?"

"Holly," Mama chided gently, "remember your manners. A person can answer only one question at a time."

Mark could honestly say he wasn't nervous. At least not yet. He told them what Mr. Schoggen had said about uniforms for the summer and about their involvement in the Fourth of July parade and the Sunday concerts.

"Just think," Carol said, "when Edward and I are picnicking in the park this summer, enjoying the music floating out from the bandstand, it may be my own little brother helping to make the music."

"Edward, Edward," Allyson said with a laugh. "Is there anything that doesn't bring Edward to your mind these days?"

Carol blushed. "I guess not," she replied. To Mark, she said, "Good luck, little brother. I feel sure you'll make it."

Mark wanted to tell her it called for much more than luck.

"May I be excused, Mama?" Allyson pushed back her chair. "I have a frightful load of studying to do this evening."

"And I have papers to grade," Carol chimed in, folding her napkin neatly by her place.

"Of course, girls," Mama told them.

"Could your work wait one moment?" Christopher asked. "I have a bit of good news to tell."

"Tell us!" Holly said. "I love good news."

"I've found a publishing house who's interested in my novel."

"Why, Christopher," Mama said, "that's wonderful news. Why didn't you tell me sooner?"

"I wanted to tell all of you at once." He smiled as he looked around the table. "All of my family!"

Holly fairly bounced in her chair. "We're so proud of you. When will it be published? I want to take it to school and show everyone!"

Christopher laughed at Holly's excitement. Mark liked his stepfather's laugh. It was a ready laugh—an easy laugh.

"Hold on a minute, Holly," Christopher answered. "The editor likes it, but it's not purchased yet. Revisions are needed."

"You mean you have to work on it more?" Holly asked.

"That's what revision means," Carol put in, using her school-teacher voice.

The novel Christopher was talking about was one he had written a few years ago and had been trying without success to sell. Now he had a chance. Mark agreed that it was very exciting—for all of them. Not because he wanted to show off Christopher's books at school, but simply because good things were happening for his stepfather. Mark liked the way Christopher said "my family." The words gave Mark a good feeling deep down inside.

"I'll have my nose to my typewriter even more in the next few months," he told them. "I hope you'll understand."

"Of course, dear," Mama said in her kindest voice. "We'll respect your need for quiet as much as we possibly can."

After supper, Mark went to his room with the lilting melody of "Peacherine Rag" dancing through his head. One wall of his room was plastered with many photos of Mr. Sousa, but there the similarity between his room and Jens's ended. Mark's room was much nicer, with its flowered wallpaper, chintz curtains, and soft rugs.

Down the hall was the family bathroom with a roomy porcelain bathtub and a real water closet. Jens's family still used an outhouse in the alley. But things like that didn't make any difference between good friends. And they *were* good friends, in spite of all that had been happening.

Mark opened his case and oiled the keys on his trumpet, working them up and down. Then he set up his music stand, spread out the pages of music, and began to practice. He began with the scales, then moved on to the exercises Mr. Schoggen had assigned. Just as he was starting on the piece for commencement that contained his solo, he heard the front door open and close.

Stepping away from the music stand, he looked out the window in time to see Christopher walking down the sidewalk. He was wearing his hat and coat, his shoulders were hunched, and his hands jammed in his pockets. His fast pace made it appear that he was in a hurry to get away from the house.

Mark watched for a moment, then sat down on his bed to think. Could it have been his practicing that had driven Christopher from his typewriter? If so, how was he ever going to practice to be good enough for the summer brass band?

CHAPTER 4

Band Auditions

Everyone in the front parlor wore funny paper hats, even Mama and Aunt Elise. It was May 15, 1906, Mark's thirteenth birthday. Aunt Elise, Uncle Abe, and Maureen had come to help celebrate. Everyone was there except Peter, who couldn't make it home in the middle of the week. However, his term at the university in Rochester was nearly over. Then he'd be home for the entire summer. Mark could hardly wait for his older brother to be home once again. Things were never the same without Peter around.

Mark would have liked to have invited Jens to the party, but ever since Father died four years ago, birthday parties had become small family affairs. There'd been no funds for big parties.

Holly sat at the piano playing "Happy Birthday," and everyone joined in singing to Mark. Maureen and Uncle Abe both held paper crackers behind their backs. At the end of the last strains of the song, they pulled the crackers to make them pop and explode, sending the others into gales of laughter.

Carol and Allyson hugged Mark and fussed about how tall he was getting. Mama hugged him and said how she wished Father could see him now.

For his birthday dinner, Stella had prepared his favorite, roast duck, and after they'd all stuffed themselves, they came into the parlor to gather around the piano and sing. Holly opened the blue *Brewer's Collection of Popular Songs,* and together they sang:

Mid pleasures and palaces though we may roam,
Be it ever so humble, there's no place like home;
A charm from the skies seems to hallow us there,
Which, seek thro' the world, is ne'er met with
elsewhere.

Christopher came over to Mama and Mark and put his big arms about the two of them as his voice rose louder than the rest on the chorus:

Home, home, sweet, sweet home,
There's no place like home,
Oh, there's no place like home.

Mark knew Christopher was pleased and proud to have them as his family and to have this home as his home. The joy was written all over his face.

All through the pages of the blue book they went, singing song after song, from "Annie Laurie" and "The Blue Bells of Scotland" to "Those Evening Bells" and "Comin' Thro' the Rye." Uncle Abe's favorites were the rounds. He liked to pit Christopher, Mark, and himself against all the ladies, saying, "We men with our powers of concentration can keep our parts better than the women." But then he would laugh and lose his place every time.

Presently Mama said, "Enough of the singing. Time for gifts to be opened." Carol and Allyson led Mark to the love seat by the curio cabinet and sat him down. Holly and Maureen had slipped from the room, then miraculously there appeared several wrapped packages on the nearby table.

Mark ripped off strings and tore open paper. There were new shirts from Mama and a box of nice white handkerchiefs from Allyson and Carol—on which they had monogrammed his initials in bright blue. Holly had purchased sheet music of new songs for him to play. Christopher gave him a recording of Sousa's "The Invincible Eagle" to play on the gramophone. "Thank you," Mark kept saying as he opened each gift. "Thank you, all."

Then Maureen stepped forward with a small package. This past year at school, his adopted cousin had suddenly seemed much older than Mark—almost as old as Allyson. They'd been inseparable friends when they were younger, but now Mark sometimes felt awkward around Maureen. She smiled as she handed him the gift. "Mother and Father and I," she said in her soft Irish brogue, "wanted to give this to a young man who spends so much time thinking."

Mark couldn't imagine what she meant. But as soon as the wrapping fell away, he got her drift. They had given him a bound leather-covered book of blank pages. Inside the front cover in Maureen's neat penmanship was written: *To Mark Morgan on his 13th birthday. Sort out your thoughts on these pages, and then your mind won't have to carry them all. Love from Cousin Maureen, Aunt Elise, and Uncle Abe.*

Even though Mark politely thanked them for the journal, he couldn't imagine ever writing in it. He'd never even thought of keeping a journal before. It seemed a boring thing to do. Nothing that happened to him would ever be worth writing about.

Mama then gave him an envelope. The handwriting on the outside belonged to Peter. "Peter wanted me to give this to you at your birthday party," she said.

Inside was a greeting card that sent happy birthday wishes. There was also a photograph of Peter standing outside an ivy-covered brick building on the university campus. The note inside told Mark how Peter wished he could be there to help celebrate. *But I'll definitely be on hand to hear your solo at the commencement services,* he wrote. He went on to say:

> *I've been given an incredible opportunity to work in the biology laboratory on campus through the summer, so I won't be staying with all of you this year. I'll miss everyone terribly, as I do every day. But my professor has opened this door for me and I cannot say no.*

The words made Mark swallow hard. Peter was not coming home. More months without him around. The thought gave Mark a lonely feeling. He looked up at Mama. "Peter says he's not coming home for the summer."

Mama nodded. "Yes, Mark, I know. But I felt you should hear it from him."

"Well, come on everyone," Uncle Abe said. "Let's let the expert driver take us for a ride in the Oldsmobile. The expert driver being the birthday boy, of course."

That invitation was enough to make Mark forget about Peter for the time being. He liked nothing better than to drive Uncle Abe's newest automobile. After the ladies were decked out in their long motoring coats and their faces draped with veils, Mark deftly drove through the winding streets of Fair Oaks, honking the horn as he went.

Several of the neighbors enjoying the spring evening on their front porches waved and smiled. Some called out their greetings. It was growing dusk, but the electric headlamps lit the road ahead as though it were broad daylight. Driving the motor car gave Mark a feeling of freedom and adventure, which he loved.

That night before going to bed, he decided—out of politeness to Maureen—to write something in the journal. He wrote: *I am now thirteen years old. I thought I would feel different, but I don't. Peter's not staying home for the summer. Uncle Abe let me drive his motor car.*

It didn't look like much, but that would have to do for now.

On the Friday following Mark's birthday, Mr. Schoggen had the schedule of audition times that had been sent to him by Mr. Klawinski. When Mark learned that each school had been assigned separate days, he was relieved. He'd thought he would have to audition in front of students from other schools whom he did not know. Being there with his friends would make it easier to relax.

At least that's the way it seemed at first. However, when

audition day finally arrived, Mark's entire midsection was tied in knots.

After school, nine boys from the Fair Oaks band walked together up Hennepin Avenue with music cases in hand to the Rose Drugstore. Mr. Anson Rose was a member of the band, and after his family had moved from the upstairs apartment to a house on the outskirts of town, he gave the upstairs over to the brass band for their rehearsal hall.

When the boys arrived at the small door beside the drug-store that led to the stairwell, no one wanted to open the door first. They stood looking at one another.

Suddenly Harvey said, "What's the matter. Are you all lily-livered?"

"Everyone's a little nervous," said Leo, the flutist in the group.

"Aw, there's nothing to be nervous about. We'll just play our instruments like we always do," Harvey protested.

Mark agreed with Leo about being nervous. His mouth was so dry he felt as though he'd been eating sawdust.

"If you're so confident," Leo said to Harvey, "then you open the door and lead the way."

Giving a silly bow, Harvey said, "I believe I'll do just that." He opened the door and started up the dim, narrow stairs. The others followed. At the top of the stairs they followed Harvey down a hallway until they came into a large room filled with folding chairs and music stands.

Mark could see where several walls had been removed to create one large room for the band rehearsals. Two smaller rooms were used for storing music, instruments, and uniforms. At a desk filled with musical scores, music books, and a couple boxes of clarinet reeds sat Victor Klawinski himself. Mark had only seen the band leader from a distance, and of course always in his uniform. Now the man was in his shirt sleeves.

Looking up from the desk, he greeted the boys. "Come right on in," he said, standing up and grabbing his suit jacket from the nearby coat rack. "You're the group from Fair Oaks, I take it."

Suddenly all of them became tongue-tied. Mark took off his hat and bumped Jens, motioning for him to do the same. The others followed suit.

"Well," said Mr. Klawinski with a chuckle, "perhaps you play better than you can talk. Hang up your hats, take out your instruments, and tune up."

In a moment, as the boys were playing the scales and trying to relax, the conductor asked each one of them their names. The man stood taller than Mark remembered him, and he had clear blue eyes that twinkled as he talked. His dark hair was thick and wavy and parted cleanly down the center. His mustache was waxed and curled neatly on the ends.

"Now then," he said in a kindly tone, "how about playing something all of you know."

Feeling at ease with the man, Mark said, "We're memorizing 'The Thunderer' for school commencement."

"Good." Taking his baton from the director's stand, Mr. Klawinski said, "Let's take it from the beginning."

It was difficult to play without having the entire band around them, and especially without the bass drum to keep rhythm. And Mr. Klawinski's directing style was much different from Mr. Schoggen's. Harvey's clarinet squawked and squealed a couple times, and that made him and Jens both snicker, but Mr. Klawinski acted as though it never happened.

After they'd played that number, he listened to each one of them play something alone—something of their choosing. Mark played the solo that he would play at the concert. He'd been practicing it faithfully every day and went through it without a flaw.

In spite of Mr. Klawinski's kindness, all of them were relieved when they were told the audition was over. Back out on the street, they split up to go their various ways. Jens asked Mark if he could come over, but since it was late, Mark said he'd better go on home. He knew Stella would have supper on the table.

When he arrived home, however, Mama and Holly were not there. Heading for the kitchen, he found Stella busily rolling out dough to make noodles for chicken soup. "Hello, Stella. Where is everyone?" he asked. The house seemed quiet and empty.

"Good afternoon, Mark. Hungry?"

"Very." And he was. After all, trying out for the brass band had been quite an ordeal.

"Supper'll be ready soon, but have an orange or two in the meantime." She pushed a wisp of dark hair from her face and waved toward the fruit bowl.

Grabbing an orange and taking it to the sink to peel it, he said, "Has Mama gone shopping?"

"Your Mama and Holly have gone down to the mission to help your aunt Elise."

"To the mission?"

"Don't you remember? Your mama asked your aunt all about her work the other night at your birthday party."

"Sort of." Mark leaned against the butcher-block table and thought a moment. Ever since they'd come back from San Francisco, Mama had talked about doing something to help others. He figured it was because of all she'd seen of people helping one another after the earthquake. But why she wanted to do such a thing, Mark wasn't sure. After all, she had her own family to care for—wasn't that enough?

"Mr. Wilkins is in his study, and Carol and Allyson are in their rooms," Stella added, even though Mark hadn't asked where they were.

"When will Mama be home?"

Stella cut the thin dough in sections, piled the sections one upon the other, and then sliced the noodles in narrow strips. "Soon. She said they weren't to stay long. They were planning to look around today. The assigned work will come later."

"And Holly went along?" Mark couldn't imagine Holly wanting to go into that awful slum area.

"That she did," Stella replied. "Says she hopes her aunt Elise will let her help in the orphanage there."

Mark took another bite from a dripping orange section and swiped juice from his chin. He wished Stella would ask him about the audition, but she probably didn't even remember he was to have it.

"Better take your things to your room and wash up," she told him. "Supper will be ready directly." Lifting the breadboard, she dumped the noodles into the boiling pot of soup.

"Yes, ma'am."

In his room, Mark put his books and horn case on his bed, then took out his journal. Sitting at his desk, he opened to the next blank page and wrote: *Dear. . .*

Mark sat and stared at the word for a moment. He didn't want to write *Dear Diary*. That sounded too much like a girl. But it seemed as though the journal needed a name. Peter's middle name was Michael, which had been Father's middle name as well. Plus, Michael was the name of a very important archangel in the Bible. Michael. It had a nice sound to it. A strong sound. Like a friend who would keep your secrets for you and never tell. He started again:

Dear Michael:

I wanted to tell someone about my audition for the brass band, but since no one is around to listen, I guess I will tell you about it. I was very nervous, but I played my best. Harvey Newmire acted as though he were not nervous, but he made several bad squeaks on his clarinet.

I want very much to be in the brass band for the summer. Mr. Klawinski is kind and not at all gruff like I thought he'd be. I believe I would learn a great deal about music by studying under him.

I have to give a talk in school about San Francisco. I don't want to because Jens says I'm showing off. And also because I don't like standing in front of everyone.

Mark started to sign it as though it were a letter, but then decided against it. He looked at the writing for a moment. It felt rather good to have been able to say what he felt. And reading what he'd written about the brass band helped him to realize how much he really wanted to be a part of that group. Perhaps one day he would attend a music school and play with a famous band like Mr. John Philip Sousa's.

Just then, he heard the front door open and heard voices. Good! Mama and Holly were finally home!

CHAPTER 5

Letters to Michael

Mark's talk on San Francisco was scheduled for just a few days before commencement. The more he thought about it, the more he dreaded it. He'd tossed around a number of ideas to try to get out of it, but nothing worked.

Finally the perfect solution came to him. He would mount the photographs on sheets of pasteboard, then let the kids file by and look at them. As they filed past, he would talk. That way they would be looking at the photographs and not at him. The plan pleased him immensely.

After mounting the photos, he wrapped the sheets of pasteboard in brown paper and tied it securely with string. That way no one could see them ahead of time. He felt almost happy as he carried the unwieldy package into school and put it in the cloakroom.

When Miss Ronan called on him during history, he brought out the package, unwrapped it, and placed the sheets of pasteboard in the chalk trays of the blackboard.

"I've mounted the photographs so everyone can see them," he said to Miss Ronan. "The class can file past and look at them."

"A good idea," Miss Ronan agreed. "I'm sure you don't want everyone handling your photographs. All right, class," she said. "Stand by your desks and come forward one row at a time."

As they came, Mark stood to the side and began to talk about the train trip, the people he'd met on the train, the city of San Francisco, and then the nightmarish earthquake and fires. Everything was perfect, until Jens walked by. Under his breath, he whispered to Mark, "Pride goeth before a fall, Mr. Showoff."

"Jens Kubek," Miss Ronan said firmly, "we are to be listeners while a speaker is addressing the class."

When everyone was seated, Miss Ronan asked that Mark remain at the front while questions were asked. Mostly they wanted to know if he was afraid when the earthquake hit and what it was like afterward. Putting that experience into words was almost impossible, so he told it as briefly as possible.

After school, Mark had to go straight home with the photographs. "That's all right," Jens told him. "Harvey's invited me to his house. We're going to practice our clarinets together."

Harvey stepped up just then. "Great photographs, Mark. You wanna come over to my house to practice with us after school?"

How Mark wished Harvey would take his weasel face and go away. "I can't come today," Mark said as politely as he could. "Maybe another time."

"Yeah. Another time would probably be better," Harvey

agreed. He and Jens walked off together, leaving Mark alone.

Most Sundays, Mark wished Jens's family attended the same church as the Morgans. But this Sunday, he was rather glad they didn't. Mark needed time away from Jens to think about what was happening.

That particular morning, the pastor's sermon was about David and Saul and how David's harp music soothed the tormented Saul. Pastor pointed out how important music is in our lives and how God gave the gift of music for His children to enjoy.

"David was such a lover of music," Pastor told them, "that he played his harp out in the fields while tending his father's sheep. We know that this musician wrote many of the psalms, which are songs. The musicians of that day were armed with the songs of David."

In his mind's eye, Mark could see David out on the hillside playing his heart out with no one to bother him. No one to hinder his practice. No wonder he became so skillful.

Sometimes Mark wished he had a quiet hillside somewhere. He wasn't sure that his practice sessions were soothing to anyone in their household. But he was sure of one thing. Band music in the park or in a concert or in a parade made many people very happy. He very much wanted his music to make people happy!

Sunday afternoons were nearly always spent at Uncle Abe's house. When Mark was younger, the families had gathered at Grandmother and Grandfather Stevenson's. But his grandparents had been gone for a number of years now, and their big house had been sold.

Uncle Abe liked to talk about many interesting things over Sunday dinner. This day the subject was flying machines. "Langley's Aerodrome wouldn't have been such a dismal failure," he was saying, "if only he'd gone about his research as thoroughly as Orville and Wilbur Wright did. Now there are two men who are thorough in research. They go after flying just like Edison went after the lightbulb. They just keep getting better and better."

They were all sitting around the large mahogany table that used to sit in Grandmother Tina's dining room. An extra place had been set for Edward Weidner, Carol's beau. Edward had just passed his bar exam and was a junior partner in a local law firm. Mark didn't think Edward would make a very good attorney, because he never talked much. All he ever seemed to want to do was stare at Carol.

"Do you think you'll ever go up in an airship, Uncle Abe?" Allyson asked.

"Absolutely." His reply was full of conviction. "In fact, most of us here could very well be riding airships from city to city just like we ride in automobiles now. I believe it'll happen in our lifetime."

Christopher shook his head. "I'm not too sure about that," he said. "The *New York Times* reported it would be hundreds of years before an airship could carry humans safely across the skies. Why Samuel Langley and most of the others like him just make laughingstocks of themselves. They make a big production of launching these flights, and then they crash."

Uncle Abe helped himself to another big slice of apple pie, then said, "Just think what they were saying about the automobile only a few years ago, Christopher. They said it would never catch on. Now I understand an automobile dealer will open his business right here in the city after New Year's. And old Duffy Midlander tells me he's planning to set up a filling station where I can drive right up to get my fuel instead of keeping a barrel and a funnel in my backyard."

"That's all well and good," Christopher answered, "but rolling an automobile along the ground is nothing like keeping an airship in the air."

Mark wanted to agree with Uncle Abe. He felt sure the airships would only get better and better in the same way the automobiles were. But today he didn't feel much like jumping into the midst of a conversation. His mind was still on Jens.

Later that afternoon, he and Maureen and Holly were in the parlor playing records on the gramophone and looking at pictures through the stereograph. Maureen and Holly had been discussing the children at the orphanage. Mark tried to ignore them. Ever since Holly had visited the mission and the orphanage with Mama, she and Maureen seemed to have more to talk about. Mark felt left out.

"What would you like to hear now, Mark?" Maureen asked as she looked through the record albums.

"He only likes Sousa," Holly said.

That wasn't exactly true, but Mark didn't answer. He sorted through the box of stereograph pictures for the ones of Yellowstone Park. The geysers, waterfalls, and hot springs were fascinating to look at.

"Sousa it is then," Maureen replied, pulling a disk from the sleeve of the album page. "How about 'El Capitan'?"

"Fine," Mark said, not looking up from the amazing photo of Old Faithful.

After cranking the handle and placing the needle carefully on the record, Maureen came over to where Mark was sitting. "Sure and you're a quiet lad today," she said softly. "Could it be something's wrong?"

Mark just shrugged and switched the picture to one of a bear standing on its hind feet. It sure was a big old bear. Maybe a grizzly.

44

Mark remembered back to the time right after Father died, when he and Maureen used to spend long hours together and could talk about most everything. Those days seemed to be over. He couldn't explain it, but it was different now.

"Mark's always sullen these days," Holly put in. "A regular sourpuss. No fun at all."

"Now, now, Holly. It's no fair to talk that way about your brother when you don't know if something's bothering him or not."

"Oh something's bothering him all right," Holly said. "He's wooling around in his mind what he'll look like all gussied up in a band uniform this summer. That, or he's worried about his solo at commencement."

"Is that it, Mark?" Maureen asked. "Your solo? Don't forget, I have to give a speech at commencement. I admit I'm a little nervous as well." She patted his shoulder. "You'll do fine. Just fine."

Mark heaved a sigh. "Thank you, Maureen," he said.

That evening before going to sleep, Mark began writing in his journal and couldn't seem to stop. He confided to Michael how he wished Peter were coming home for the summer, how he wished he could talk to Maureen like they used to in the old days, how he wished Mama didn't care a thing about the mission and working with Aunt Elise. He even told how he wished Christopher weren't so busy with his novel. If he had said any of those things out loud to anyone, he would have sounded like a whining baby. But Michael kept the secrets and helped him sort out his jumbled thoughts.

It was sort of like talking to Maureen. After all, she'd been the one to give him the journal in the first place.

CHAPTER 6

Audition Results

The night of commencement, noise filled the backstage room. Band students talked and laughed as they tuned up their instruments. Excitement surged through the room like electrical sparks. Mr. Schoggen struggled to bring order to the room and give last-minute instructions. Mark was especially excited because his brother Peter was in the audience.

"There's one more thing I'd like to tell you," Mr. Schoggen said, adjusting his glasses. "We have a special guest in the audience. Mr. Klawinski decided to come and listen to our concert."

Mark's stomach turned a somersault, and his stiffly starched collar felt even tighter.

"Those of you who auditioned for the summer brass band will want to do your very best. Just take a deep breath and focus on the music and on my directions, and you'll do fine."

Just then the door opened and another teacher announced, "It's time."

Mr. Schoggen motioned for them to rise. They stood and filed out of the room, through the side curtain of the stage, and down the steps to the chairs that had been set up for them in front of the stage. A hush fell over the audience. A seventh-grade girl played the piano softly. Mr. Schoggen stepped to his podium and lifted his baton. The band members raised their instruments and began to play.

As soon as the music started, the eighth-grade graduating class entered from the back of the auditorium and came slowly down the two aisles. Mark glanced away from Mr. Schoggen for a fraction of a moment to catch a glimpse of Maureen as she came down the aisle. She looked prettier than Mark had ever seen her. How she'd changed from the shy little daughter of a hired cook to the adopted daughter of Uncle Abe and Aunt Elise. Mark was very proud of her. Because she had the best grades in her class, Maureen was to give the opening address.

When her time came, she spoke with confidence and clarity about the role women would play in this new century. She cited quotations from outstanding women leaders, including Francis Willard, Elizabeth Cady Stanton, and Susan B. Anthony. Then she described in detail the work of Jane Addams at the famous Hull House in Chicago. From there, she described her own two adoptive parents and the tireless hours they poured into the Y.M.C.A., the orphanage, the mission, and the settlement houses in the city.

In closing, she told the audience, "All that I am and all that I will ever become, I owe to these two loving people who took me in and loved me upon the death of my dear mother almost four years ago. Thank you Mother and Father—Mr. and Mrs. Abraham Stevenson." When she concluded, there wasn't a dry eye in the entire auditorium.

At different times throughout the program, the band played. Mark's solo, however, wasn't until the very end—the finale—which gave his nervousness a chance to grow as the evening progressed.

Finally, all the special awards, presentations, and speeches were completed. Mr. Schoggen received a nod from the master of ceremonies up on the stage. He then lifted his baton and the finale began.

Many times, Mr. Schoggen had told them, "When it comes time to play, for you there will be no audience, no pressure to perform correctly, there will be only the music, the orchestra, and your conductor. If you allow it to do so, the music will come and capture you and carry you away."

That evening as Mark stood to play his solo, it happened. Every ounce of nervousness he'd wrestled with all evening simply melted away. His breathing was free. He came up under the notes and sent them out pure and clear. By keeping his eyes on Mr. Schoggen it was easy to pretend there was no audience. Mr. Schoggen's face grew flushed as he waved the baton in perfect rhythm. Then came the crescendo, and Mark's trumpet sounded the notes above all the rest. The cymbals crashed, and the drums pounded. Suddenly, it was over. The audience was on their feet. Mark sat down, beaming.

When the benediction was pronounced, Mark was suddenly surrounded by his family. They fussed over him and congratulated him. Peter gave him a firm handshake and with a big smile said, "I just can't believe what a good musician you've become, Mark. What wonderful things you can do with that horn."

Then Mr. Schoggen motioned to Mark. By Mr. Schoggen's side stood Mr. Klawinski. The conductor of the brass band said, "I just wanted to come up and say hello." He looked around. "Where are the other boys who auditioned?"

Mark quickly gathered the other boys and brought them over. Mr. Klawinski greeted each one by name and shook their hands. As he did, he congratulated each on a job well done. What a compliment that was!

Mark hoped Mr. Klawinski would tell them whether or not they'd made it into the band, but he didn't. Mr. Schoggen told them the formal announcements would come by letter. "However," he added after Mr. Klawinski had left, "it's a good sign that he wanted to hear you play in front of an audience."

Later, the family crowded into Uncle Abe's Oldsmobile, and he drove them to Bailey's Confectionery, where they all ordered fruit concentrate sodas. Mark drank greedily through a paper straw. The cool sweet drink felt wonderful on his parched throat.

As they talked and laughed, Maureen teased him about upstaging her speech with his great solo. The compliment made him blush. But he knew her speech had been wonderful, and she hadn't sounded one bit nervous.

The graduated eighth graders came back to school the following Monday to pick up their report cards and go home. But the rest of the students had another dreary week of classes. That alone made Mark wish he were a year older.

What made it worse was that Peter was home. Mark begged Mama to let him skip those last days in order to be with Peter, but Mama said absolutely not. "If school is in session, you are to be in school," she told him. "And you'll have every evening with Peter."

Evenings, however, were much too short. Peter spent much time talking with Mama, Carol, and Allyson. At mealtime, Peter sat next to Christopher, and they talked about everything from biology to politics to family matters.

At times Mark felt like a child whose opinions didn't count for anything. He knew no one meant to make him feel that way, but the feelings didn't go away. Mark overheard Peter telling Mama how pleased he was that Christopher was now part of the family and was there to take care of everyone. Mark wished he could explain to everyone that while Christopher was a good stepfather, it was still lonely without Peter.

In spite of what Mama had said about being in school, she did allow Mark to miss an hour of school on Wednesday morning as they took Peter to the train station. Carol had another teacher take care of her students so she, too, could be at the station. Allyson skipped a class and Christopher pried himself away from his novel, so everyone was there.

Peter hugged his three sisters and Mama. He shook hands with Christopher, then came to Mark. Mark could remember when Peter had seemed like a giant. Now they stood nearly eye-to-eye. Yet Mark wished he could throw himself into Peter's arms and cling to him like he used to when he was younger.

"It's amazing to watch you becoming a young man right in front of my eyes," Peter said as he thrust out his hand to shake Mark's. Mark put his hand into Peter's and blinked back burning tears.

"I'm proud of you, little brother," Peter told him. "Very proud of you." With that he clasped his free hand on Mark's shoulder and pulled him into a gigantic bear hug, knocking Mark's hat to the ground. When he was released, Mark saw he wasn't the only one with wet eyes. Peter pulled out his handkerchief and blew his nose.

"I'll have more time to be with you when I come home in August," Peter said to Mark. "We'll do something—just you and I."

"Thanks," Mark managed to mumble.

The call of the conductor ended the conversation. Grabbing his valise, Peter hopped aboard, waving from the window as soon as he was seated. After the huffing train had pulled away from the station, Mark and Holly caught the trolley to go to school.

The last day of school turned out to be very warm. The heat made everyone twice as thankful that it was the final day. Mark somehow felt that even the teachers were glad. How could anyone bear to attend school in the heat of summer?

That afternoon, as they filed into the stuffy band room, Mark wondered when they would ever hear about Mr. Klawinski's decision. While they were tuning up, Mr. Schoggen praised them on the fine job they'd done throughout the school year and thanked them for their dedication and hard work.

They ran through a few of the numbers that last September had been anything but smooth. Now they sounded quite good. When class was over, Mr. Schoggen asked the candidates for summer brass band to remain behind. Mark felt his breath catch in his throat.

Soon the room was empty except for the nine boys who had auditioned. Mr. Schoggen invited them to sit down in the front row of the practice area. He went to his desk, picked up a sheet of paper, and stood in front of them.

"I now have Mr. Klawinski's decisions," he told them. "I want you to know I'm proud of each of you for trying out. I admire your courage and your desire to learn more about band music. In Mr. Klawinski's letter, he says it was extremely difficult to choose among the candidates. He could only take fifteen applicants in the whole city, and of course he had to have a variety of instruments. That made it even more difficult."

"Please, Mr. Schoggen," Jens spoke up, "could you just tell us who made it and who didn't?"

Mr. Schoggen laughed. "I apologize. I didn't mean to drag it out. I just wanted you to know the circumstances." In alphabetical order he began calling off the names of those who made it. Mark heard him say "Jens Kubek," but after he said, "Mark Morgan," Mark heard nothing else.

Fireworks exploded inside of him. He wanted to jump up and holler as loud as he could and run down the school hallway shouting to everyone that he'd made it. Him. Plain old Mark Morgan would be wearing a uniform with gold braid and brass buttons. He would be marching in the Fourth of July parade. He would be studying under a master musician and conductor. He could hardly believe it was true.

He wasn't even sure whose names had not been called. He felt badly for them, but it was hard to sort out those feelings when he was so excited. Jens and Harvey were punching one another, so he knew Harvey had made it as well.

"I'll expect you to behave responsibly," Mr. Schoggen was saying, "and be fine representatives of Fair Oaks Elementary School. That's all boys. You're dismissed, and may God bless you."

After they were out in the hallway, Mark realized that five of the boys had not made it. Only four were in. His head was still spinning as he went to his last class.

At last the long hot day was over and they walked out the big double doors for the last time that school term. Jens, who was right at Mark's elbow, said, "Are you coming over, Mark?"

"Not today," Mark said. "I want to hurry home and tell Mama that I made it into the brass band."

"Well, after you tell her, why don't you come over to Harvey's house. We're gonna be practicing together."

"I'll see," he called back as he hurried down the sidewalk. He could hardly wait to see the look on Mama's face when he told her.

Holly and Maureen were walking along with a cluster of girls. As he ran past them, he said, "Did you hear my good news? I made it into the brass band!"

The girls all cheered. "I knew you could do it, Mark!" Maureen said.

"Congratulations!"

He thought that last shout came from Holly, but he was running too fast to tell for sure. Within minutes he was slamming the front door, yelling "Mama! Mama! I have great news! Mama, are you home?"

Just as he was running pell-mell down the hallway, Christopher came out of his office. "What in thunderation is all that racket?" he demanded. "How is a guy supposed to get any work done around here?"

CHAPTER 7

In the Brass Band

Mark had never heard such anger in Christopher's voice. He felt like melting into the floor.

Christopher raked his fingers through his hair, making it stand up in places. "What're you doing home so early?" he asked. "And what's all the infernal racket about?"

"It's not early. School is out."

Only then did Mark's stepfather take his watch fob from his vest pocket and look at it. "I can't believe it," he said. He went back into his office shaking his head.

Before the door closed, Mark asked, "Where's Mama?"

"With your aunt Elise." The door closed.

Just then, Stella came scuttling down the hall from the

kitchen with her finger to her lips. "Sh, Mark. Mr. Wilkins is having a terrible day. Something about his book. A part that doesn't want to cooperate, he says. Come back to the kitchen."

She put her arm about Mark's shoulders to guide him. It made him feel like a three-year-old. "I just took lemon bars from the oven. Can't you smell them?"

Once they were in the kitchen, Stella said, "It's difficult for Mr. Wilkins when he's trying to concentrate and the story isn't working right. He needs it to be very quiet, you know."

Mark wasn't sure he did know. It didn't seem right for Christopher to react with such an outburst.

"Now what was all the shouting about?" Stella wanted to know. With a wide spatula, she lifted two of the still-warm lemon bars from the pan and placed them on a plate.

"Don't bother with a plate," Mark told her. "Wrap them in a napkin, and I'll take them with me."

"Where're you going?"

"To practice my trumpet with Jens and Harvey."

"But your Mama. . ."

"I won't be long," he said, taking the napkin, which was warm and heavy with the aroma of lemon.

"But your news," she said.

"I guess it can wait." And he was out the door.

Mark had never been to Harvey Newmire's house. For one thing, Mark had never cared for Harvey and never wanted to be his friend. But now that Jens had taken up with him, Mark realized he'd better take a closer look. Maybe he'd been too hasty in his judgment of Harvey. At least he was willing to give it a try.

Harvey's house was in a neighborhood just the other side of the Kubek's shop. He was very nearly in the Washington

School District. The rowhouses were pressed close together, leaving little room for lawns, flowers, or shade trees. In Fair Oaks, where Mark lived, the double rows of maples on either side created a grand arch all the way down Vine Place.

When he knocked at the front door of the Newmire rowhouse, a lady came to the door dressed in baggy bloomers and a shirtwaist. Mark had often seen his aunt Elise wear her bicycle suit with the shorter skirt, and she always wore them with hightop boots. But bloomers? This was something entirely new.

"Hello," she said, "are you a friend of Harvey's?"

Mark nodded self-consciously. "I'm Mark Morgan. Jens Kubek said they would be here practicing."

"And I'm Mrs. Newmire, Harvey's mother. Won't you come in? They're in the basement," she said. He followed her down a narrow hallway that ran parallel to a staircase. As he did, he could hear the sounds of clarinets playing below. At the end of the hall, she turned to show him the stairs to the basement. They ran directly beneath the stairs to the second story.

She pulled back a curtain that hung over the doorway. "Harvey," she called. "Take a break. You have company."

Harvey stuck his head around the corner. "Hello, Mark. We were just getting started. Come on down and join in."

Mark tripped down the stairs and saw a nice room with rugs on the floor. In the far corner, the coal furnace had been walled off. The boys had music stands set up. Sheets of music were on the stands and scattered about the room.

Jens played a catchy little tune on his clarinet and made a funny face as he did so. Then he said, "It's about time you decided to come over and be with us. Get your tooter out and let's go."

Mark laughed, plopped his case down on a worn velvet settee, and snapped open the clasps. As he did, Jens said,

"Looky here, Mark. Look at the albums Harvey has."

Beside the gramophone sat a wooden orange crate full of record albums. And Mark had thought Uncle Abe had a bunch.

"Most of them are rags," Jens added.

"Is that right?" Mark asked. He went over and took a closer look. "And your parents don't care?"

"Naw," Harvey said. "My mother and father are progressive thinkers. They want me to be up on all the latest things."

"So do I," Jens echoed.

"So do you what?" Mark asked.

"So do I want to be up on all the latest things."

Mark wondered what all the latest things would include. He wasn't sure that he totally agreed with Jens. But he did have to admit, it was nice to have someone to practice with, and it was nice not to feel as though they were disturbing anyone. They practiced piece after piece. The time flew by. When Mark finally thought to ask what time it was, Harvey, who wore a nice wristwatch, said it was five-thirty.

"Oh my!" Mark quickly pulled the mouthpiece from his horn and put it and the horn in his case. "I could be in some real trouble. Mama doesn't even know where I am."

"Well, next time tell her, will ya?" Jens said.

"She wasn't at home when I got there." He started up the stairs, then turned back. "Thanks, Harvey. I had a good time." He hurried out without waiting for Mrs. Newmire to show him to the door.

As he ran toward home, he kept thinking that Mama hadn't told him she was going to be gone from the house. So why should he tell her where he was going to be? But the attempt to rationalize his behavior was futile. He could have left Harvey's name and address with Stella, but he'd been too upset with Christopher to even think of it.

Mama was indeed in a stew by the time Mark got home. She'd just called Mrs. Kubek to see if he was there. Jens's mother had given Mama the number of the Newmires', and Mrs. Newmire told Mama that Mark had just left.

Thankfully Mark got out of the mess with only a scolding. "Next time," Mama warned, "let someone know where you are and what time you'll be home."

"Yes, ma'am," he answered. Then he said, "Mama, I made it into the brass band. I'm going to be studying under Mr. Klawinski all summer."

"Yes, I know," she said. "Holly told me. I'm very proud of you, Son."

Holly told? Well, of course she would have told. After all, he was gone when Mama came home, and he never told Holly to keep it a secret. Still, there was a nasty, sour feeling inside him because the fun of breaking the exciting news had been spoiled.

That night, Christopher didn't come to the dinner table. He asked Stella to bring him a sandwich in his study. Good for him, Mark thought. After the way his stepfather had exploded, he ought to stay in his room all evening!

Before he went to sleep that night, Mark spilled all his hurt feelings onto the pages in his letter to Michael. At the end he wrote:

> *If only Mama had been home when I came in after school, nothing bad would have happened. I don't see why she has to spend all that time at the orphanage anyway. We need her right here.*

The first practice with the brass band was an adventure, a challenge, and a joy all wrapped up in one package. Mr.

Schoggen's strictest days paled in comparison with what Mr. Klawinski demanded of his musicians at each and every rehearsal. He expected nothing less than their best in attitude, in attention, and in musical ability. If a certain measure did not please him, they played it over and over until it was smooth as silk.

"Perish the thought that we are simply a part-time group meeting above a drugstore, struggling to cobble a few songs together," he told them. "Our band can be, and will be, second to none. Except, perhaps, for Mr. Sousa's concert band."

That comment made Mark glance at Jens, and they exchanged smiles. It was no secret that Mr. Sousa had the best band in the entire world.

The junior members were allowed to be a part of rehearsals all during June, but they would not join in the concerts until July Fourth. That great citywide holiday would be their "coming out" day. On Saturday mornings, the brass band members met in the park and practiced marching. It was quite a trick to be able to march in step and play music at the same time.

Mark had prepared himself for teasing from the older, more experienced members, but it never happened. He wondered if Mr. Klawinski had instructed them to be helpful, because to a man, they lent support and assistance to the junior members. And when mistakes were made—which happened quite often—there was no laughing or teasing from the veterans.

Many of the band members were Jewish. Mark didn't know any Jewish children, and he enjoyed getting to know these men, many of whom had come to America to escape persecution in Europe.

Mr. Klawinski never failed to begin each and every rehearsal with a prayer asking God to help them to do their very best. "We never want to forget to give glory to the One who gave us our talents," he told them.

The older Jewish men would nod, smile, stroke their beards, and say, "*Omaine,*" in hearty agreement.

On the first night of rehearsals, the junior members had been measured from head to toe for their band uniforms. Late in June, following a particularly grueling rehearsal, Mr. Klawinski said, "Junior members, please report to the storeroom before leaving. I have packages for each of you."

Mark's heart beat double time. It had to be their uniforms. In just a few short minutes, the room was filled with talking, laughing boys. They tore at the brown paper and string. Soon the boys were holding up navy-colored jackets to check arm length and setting their military-style caps jauntily on their heads.

Older members stood back out of the way, enjoying the excitement almost as much as the younger ones. Mark ran his fingers over the lightweight wool fabric, traced the swirls of the bright gold braid, and admired the shiny bill on the cap. He picked up the britches and held them up to his waist to check out the length. They were perfect. Now he was ready for the Fourth of July parade.

Even though Christopher was still struggling desperately with his novel, he promised to take the entire day off for the Fourth. Mark was pleased at this announcement. He'd never realized before how much work went into one single book. Scanning the shelves at the school library, he thought of all the people who'd poured themselves into the words on the pages. Was there a lonely family behind every author? Sometimes Mark worried that Mama might be lonely because Christopher was always working on the book.

One Sunday morning, Christopher surprised the family by announcing he'd have to stay home and miss the church service. Writing when no one was in the house seemed to be the best way for him to work. "I know the book seems to be taking forever," he said, "but in fact, I'm getting closer to completion each day."

Mark could hardly imagine anyone skipping church. It didn't seem right. Mama never disagreed with Christopher in front of the children. "Whatever you think is best," she'd say. But Mark was quite certain she didn't like it.

On the morning of Independence Day, Mark was up before dawn. At seven o'clock sharp, he was to report in uniform to the park, where the parade was to begin. He hurried through the early morning coolness to Kubek's Butcher Shop. He and Harvey were meeting Jens there. Together, they would walk to Central Park.

As he opened the front door, Mark heard Mr. Kubek saying to Jens, "Plenty of German bands there are. Why you don't want to be in no German band? Eh?"

"But Papa, I was invited to play in the brass band. No German band has invited me."

"Maybe you are ashamed of being a German boy, is that it?"

They stopped talking as Mark rattled the door. "Ready, Jens?" he called out. "Good morning, Mr. Kubek."

Mr. Kubek cleared his throat noisily. "Good morning, young Mark." He turned back to his work at the counter.

"Are you going to close the shop and come watch the parade?" Jens asked his father as he picked up his clarinet case and put on his cap. Skinny though Jens was, Mark had to admit that his sandy-haired friend looked very nice in his uniform. But Mr. Kubek didn't seem to notice.

"Is only Wednesday," Mr. Kubek said stiffly. "Still customers need meat on Wednesday."

"Most businesses are closed today, Mr. Kubek," Mark offered.

"Most businesses is not Kubek's Butcher Shop," Mr. Kubek said as he swung his meat cleaver down on a slab of beef. "Beside, is not our day of independence."

"Papa," Jens said lamely, "we're Americans now. It *is* our Independence Day."

"Yours, perhaps. Not mine."

Jens looked at Mark and shrugged. The matter seemed to be closed. "Good-bye, Papa," he said as he and Mark went out the door.

Mark wanted to tell Jens how sorry he was that Jens's family would not be there for this special moment, but he didn't know how to put it into words. And besides, he could see Harvey coming down the street. Mark didn't want Harvey to hear.

Brightly decorated floats, clowns dressed in striped baggy pants, and high-stepping horses with silver bridles and saddles were jousting for position, while parade officials ran about with clipboards in their hands, attempting to bring order to the chaos. The boys quickly found their group and took their places.

Mr. Klawinski led them through several drills and gave last-minute instructions. Mark was amazed at how large the parade actually was. It seemed to take forever just to get everything in order. Even after it started, because the bands and floats moved so slowly, the wait for their turn was endless.

At last, Mr. Klawinski waved his long drum major's baton with the gold tassels on the end. The members of the brass band stood at attention. A shrill blow from his whistle, and they raised their instruments. Another signal from the whistle, the baton pointed forward, and they stepped out. They were on their way!

The parade route went up Hennepin Street, over a block on Washington to Nicollet, then down Nicollet and back to the park. The bank where Uncle Abe worked stood on Hennepin, and all of Mark's family would be watching from its second-story windows. The streets were jam-packed with people. Mark decided that all of Minneapolis must be there, along with half of St. Paul.

Mark had never felt so happy, so proud, so. . .so complete. Bringing music to people was nothing short of pure joy. The parade route was long, but he never once felt tired. He could have marched forever. As he'd been taught, Mark kept his eyes straight ahead and concentrated on the steps and rhythm. The drums and cymbals reverberated in his feet and echoed up into his heart. Only when they approached the bank on Hennepin did he let his eyes stray. He had to glance up. There they all were, waving and yelling to him. He smiled. Surely this was what he was born to do!

CHAPTER 8

Camille Wilmot

Following the parade, Mark, Jens, and Harvey strolled through the crowds in the park, enjoying the admiring glances from the pretty girls and the looks of envy from other boys.

They decided not to compete in the races and games because they had to keep their uniforms clean. That evening they would be playing a concert in the bandstand. And even though it was very hot, they never unbuttoned so much as one brass button on their coats.

Several churches were sponsoring food sales in brightly

colored tents, and the air was heavy with the wonderful aromas. Mama and Aunt Elise were working with other women from their church in a large red-and-white-striped tent, where fried chicken dinners were sold for twenty cents a plate. Parade participants, however, all had tickets for free meals. The boys filed in, handed over their tickets, and took their loaded plates to the plank tables set up inside the tent.

No sooner had they sat down than Holly, Maureen, and a group of their girlfriends came in talking and laughing together. All were dressed in frilly summer dresses and flowered hats. Even though Maureen was a full three years older than Holly, they'd become close friends, especially since Holly was now helping in the work at the mission.

"You were wonderful," Maureen said, her dark eyes wide. "More than wonderful. Wonderful and splendid!"

"You truly were very good." Holly echoed the compliment.

Mark felt his ears turning red, but the words set well.

"Is that remark just for your brother," Harvey wanted to know, "or all of us?"

Holly looked over at him. "Oh, for all of you, of course."

"Naturally," Maureen insisted. "It was amazing how one couldn't tell the junior players from the old-timers. You marched and played as well as the others."

The rest of the girls smiled and twittered their agreement.

"Thank you, Maureen," Mark said.

"Come on, girls," Holly said, "let's get our lunch. Save our places, boys."

When they were out of earshot, Harvey said in a high voice, "Save our places, boys." In his normal voice he said, "We'll certainly do that, won't we, boys? I don't see any other fellows surrounded by a bevy of girls." Then to Mark, he said, "Your sister sure is pretty!"

Mark looked over at Holly, who was almost lost in the crowd working its way toward plates of fried chicken and mashed potatoes and gravy. He studied her for a moment. She was shorter than Maureen and a bit heavier. Maureen was a classic beauty with her ivory skin and black hair. Holly, blessed with curly mousey-colored hair and green eyes like Mama's, was more plain. But pretty? It was a new thought. One that had never occurred to him before.

After they'd eaten lunch, the girls joined them at the baseball field to watch the ball game. Harvey pushed in to sit by Holly. His sister seemed to giggle nonstop while the game was going on. Mark didn't quite know what to make of it all.

To play in the bandstand that evening was a dream come true for Mark. This was different than the parade. The parade passed by quickly, and there were the sounds of other bands to contend with. But here in the bandstand with the park full of people sitting about on blankets and on benches, the Municipal Brass Band was the absolute center of attention. The elegant bandstand was an open affair with a cupola roof and large Grecian pillars. Mark had admired it for years, and now here he was sitting up inside with Mr. Klawinski's admired brass band.

They played waltzes, two-steps, and marches. The melodies swelled and floated out across the sweet summer night air. It was a perfect evening. Mark's family had spread their blankets just to the side of the bandstand, and he could glance over and see their looks of pride and admiration.

Mr. Klawinski had chosen one of Sousa's newer marches, "The Stars and Stripes Forever," as the finale. As they played the rousing march, fireworks were shot off in the air. The crowd rose to their feet and cheered and waved flags. When the last spark of the last blazing fireworks had flickered out, the crowd still wanted to hear the beautiful march played again and again.

Mark was certainly the honored one as the family rode home that evening in Uncle Abe's Oldsmobile. His family raved on and on about what a marvelous job he'd done.

Even though he was exhausted, before falling asleep that evening, he took out his journal and wrote:

Dear Michael:
    Words could never begin to describe what a perfect day this has been. Independence Day, 1906. My first time to march and play with the brass band. The event was even more glorious than I ever dreamed it could be. Playing my trumpet is more of a passion to me than I had ever before realized.

After describing as many details of the day as he could recall, he added this note:

    Oh yes, something very strange happened. Harvey Newmire said Holly is pretty. Isn't that odd?

With that, Mark put his journal away and quickly fell asleep.

After the exciting celebration on the Fourth, summer fell into a quiet routine. Mama and Holly helped Aunt Elise three afternoons a week. On the other days they went calling and attended various women's club meetings. Although Carol was not teaching during the summer months, she was taking extra classes at Normal School, so she and Allyson were both involved in books and studying.

For the most part, Mark practiced his trumpet with Harvey and Jens at Harvey's house, simply because it was easier. That way he knew he was disturbing no one at his house. But many days, Jens had to work at the butcher shop, and Mark never felt comfortable at the Newmires when Jens wasn't there.

Harvey was quite taken with ragtime music, and often he wanted to listen to the records more than he wanted to practice. At times, he would play along with the music and attempt to mimic the jazzy sounds. He explained to them that the term ragtime was due to the ragged rhythm of this type of music. Mark had to admit, Harvey knew a great deal about this new music.

But he kept thinking about how unhappy it had made Mama when she'd found out he'd been listening to such music at Jens's house. How would she feel if she knew he listened to it almost every day? One day when Mark suggested they stick with the music and exercises given to them by Mr. Klawinski, Harvey called him a "Goody Two-shoes." That didn't set well with Mark at all—especially when Jens laughed at the remark.

On rare occasions the three of them wound up at Mark's house. But because Christopher was so involved with his novel, and because Mark didn't dare risk getting in trouble again for being noisy, they never stayed there long.

Some days the boys would go to the park together. They had foot races, rolled hoops, played marbles, and tried to catch fish in the lake with their bare hands. Though Mark had a good time, he could never shake the feeling that Harvey was pushing in between him and Jens.

Mark was happiest during the hours spent in the large room above Rose Drugstore—in spite of the fact that the room was quite hot during the summer months. Mr. Klawinski would throw open all the windows and set electric oscillating fans around the room on the floor. But after an hour or so of going over and over the songs, most of the men were wringing wet with perspiration. Mark was amazed at their dedication. He wanted to be just like them.

Shortly after the Fourth of July, a beaming Carol announced that Edward had asked her to marry him. The wedding was to be at the close of summer just before school began. Mark just shook his head. He knew what that meant. All the women in the family would be running in circles with wedding arrangements.

He remembered all the big to-do over Mama and Christopher's wedding last spring. Personally he couldn't understand why they made such a fuss over a wedding. All one really needed was a preacher, a church, and two witnesses.

Through the summer, Mama talked often about the poor little children at the orphanage and what a difference she and her fellow club members were making there. Mark only half listened. It had nothing to do with him. He had enough problems of his own.

One day Mark was getting ready to meet Jens and Harvey. They were headed to the park for the afternoon. They'd decided to have their own marble tournament. He was heading for the front door, when Stella told him that Mama wanted to talk to him. Mama was out on the sunporch catching the afternoon breeze. Marbles made a noisy clicking in Mark's pocket as he walked back down the hallway.

"Mark," Mama said as he came in, "there you are. I have something to ask you." She was seated in the white wicker chaise, embroidering pastel flowers on a dresser scarf.

"You know how much work we've been doing for the mission and the orphanage this summer. But no matter how much is done, we're only a handful of women. Elise and I and our club president, Mrs. Granger, feel something needs to be done to bring the plight of these people to the attention of more people in the city."

Mark shifted from one foot to the other. He didn't see how this could possibly have anything to do with him. He was in a hurry to get outside.

"I would like for you to ask Mr. Klawinski if there is any possibility the brass band could play a benefit concert at the mission. That would get people's attention."

"*At* the mission?" Mark was incredulous. To go from the beautiful bandstand in Central Park to the dirty mission building down on skid row? What could Mama be thinking? "I couldn't. . ."

"Oh, we don't expect you to set anything up," Mama insisted. "We'd like for you to ask if he would be willing to discuss the idea, that's all. Would you do that for me, please? At your next rehearsal, if possible. We'd like to begin making plans as soon as possible."

Mark groaned inwardly. He'd be embarrassed to ask Mr. Klawinski such a thing. And anyway, he didn't want the band to do such a thing. Playing with the brass band was the only thing left that was totally his to enjoy. Now Mama wanted to mess that up as well. He didn't know what to say.

Mama didn't act as though an answer was expected. Returning to her embroidering, she said, "Just let me know what he says. I'll take it from there."

"Yes, ma'am," Mark answered. But he was frantically trying to think of some way to get out of this. He leaned down to kiss her cheek. "I'm meeting Jens and Harvey. We're going to the park for the afternoon."

"Don't be late for supper," she said. Then she added, "You might want to look in the parlor before you leave. Holly has met a new friend in the neighborhood."

70

"Yes, ma'am." Probably another girl. That's what this neighborhood needed—another girl. He sighed. Mark felt hopelessly outnumbered as it was.

Near the front door, he turned to go into the parlor. As he looked into the room, he felt as though all the air had been sucked out of his lungs. Holly was at the piano plunking out a tune, and sitting in a chair near the piano was the most beautiful girl Mark had ever seen. She turned ever so slightly to look over her shoulder at him. Her hair was a cloud of soft curls that seemed to float in whatever direction they pleased. No braids or chignons for this girl. Her laughing eyes sparkled, and a dimple appeared in each cheek as she smiled at him.

"Oh, Mark," Holly said, leaving off the unfinished song. "There you are. Come meet Camille. She's just moved to Fair Oaks. Camille Wilmot, this is my brother Mark. Mark will be in your class this fall."

Camille held out her hand and said how pleased she was to meet him. Her voice was more melodic than the piano. Mark didn't know if his legs would actually walk across the room toward this dream, but he was certain his voice would never cooperate.

Sure enough, as he stepped forward, his toe caught on the corner of the thick Persian rug, and he nearly stumbled. Pulling his hand from his pocket, he'd forgotten he was clasping his steelie. He started to reach out to shake her hand. "I'm glad to. . ." His voice croaked. Camille looked at the steelie in his hand and giggled.

"Oh, I didn't mean to. . ." But before he could get the big marble back to the pocket where it came from, it slipped from his hand. It hit the hardwood floor with a thunk, bounced a couple times, and then rolled past the piano. Mark wasn't sure whether to get the dropped marble or grab Camille's hand, which was still extended.

Holly spun around on the piano stool. "Goodness, Mark. Are you all right?"

Her words seemed to break though his fog. "I'm fine. I mean, how are you, Miss. Camille. I'm pleased to meet you." He actually did shake her hand, but he let go very quickly because it felt as though his hand were on fire, and he was sure she must have felt it, too. "Welcome to Fair Oaks," he managed to add.

"Thank you very much," she said. At least he guessed she said it. In his mind it seemed she was singing each word. "I like it here very much."

"Good. That's good," he replied, but his silly voice croaked again. His voice had become untrustworthy in recent days. Sometimes it would start out high and then go low, and sometimes vice versa. And he never knew which way it would go or when.

Mark bent down to retrieve his big marble. It had rolled all the way to the bay window.

"Mark plays the trumpet," Holly told Camille.

"He plays the trumpet *and* marbles?" Camille asked with another giggle.

"Actually I don't play marbles much anymore," Mark said. Suddenly marbles seemed a very childish game to be playing. As he knelt down to pick up the heavy steelie, he happened to glance through the lace curtains. Jens and Harvey were coming up on the porch. Oh how he wished he could somehow keep them from ever seeing Camille Wilmot. In a few minutes he knew why.

CHAPTER 9

Aeronauts and Airships

There was no way anyone could ignore the pounding at the door.

"Oh, you have company," Camille said. "Perhaps I should leave."

"It's only friends of Mark's," Holly told her. "They'll both be in eighth grade next year as well."

"Really?"

Pocketing the wayward steelie, Mark hurried to the parlor door. Maybe he could head the boys off. "We'll be going now, Holly," he said as he went out. "I'll see you at supper. Nice to meet you, Camille."

"Mark Morgan," Holly scolded as she came toward him.

"Aren't you at least going to introduce Camille to your friends?"

"Sure. Sure I was. It's just that. . ."

But Holly was pushing past him to the door. She politely greeted both Harvey and Jens, then invited them into the parlor to meet Camille.

Like a Broadway star stepping on stage, Jens Kubek became a different person right before Mark's eyes. Not waiting to be introduced, he strode right over to Camille, put out his hand, and said, "Hello, there. My name is Jens Kubek. I take it you're new around here." He didn't even stumble over the corner of the Persian rug.

Harvey was introduced as well, but he wasn't able to take an inch of ground. Jens had already staked claim. Within a few minutes, Jens knew what Camille's father did, where they'd moved from, and what her favorite flavor of soda was.

"I play a clarinet in the brass band," he told her. "I'll be playing in the concert in the bandstand at Central Park on Sunday afternoon. In uniform, of course. Be sure to come by and say hello. I always have a break now and then—during which time I can show you around the park."

He didn't bother to say that all three of them played in the brass band. Mark could hardly believe his friend's audacity. And Harvey was no help at all. Harvey had started talking to Holly.

Camille smiled at Jens, and her captivating dimples appeared. "Thank you for the kind invitation," she said. "I'll tell Mother and Father, and perhaps we can come."

"Hadn't we better be going?" Mark said. "The day is getting away from us."

Jens looked up at Mark. "Why don't you two go on along to the park. I'll catch up later."

An anger Mark had never experienced smoldered in his midsection and burned all the way up to his ears. At that moment if he'd made a move, he might very well have knocked Jens clear off his chair.

"Oh, don't stay back on my account," Camille said sweetly. "I was just leaving."

Jens stood then and politely expressed his regret at her having to go. Jens's tone made Mark want to throw up.

"I'll walk you back to your house," Holly said. The girls put on their summer straw hats and out the door they went.

Once the three boys arrived in the park, they didn't talk much. And no one wanted to play marbles.

That evening, Mark wrote in his journal:

Dear Michael: Tonight I'm different. I met a girl who is new to Fair Oaks. Her name is as beautiful as she is—Camille.

He studied the name. Then he wrote it in the margin of the page several times to watch the swirls of the *l*s. Everything about each letter was all curvy and flowing.

She's probably about the prettiest girl I've ever seen in my life. She doesn't wear her hair all tight and braided. It fluffs up into curls around her face, sort of like a cloud. When she smiles, there are pretty dimples in her cheeks. I was just getting to know her when Jens came and horned in, acting like a hotshot. I hope she and Holly become good friends. That way I'll see her a lot more often than Jens ever would.

I wonder if this is how Edward feels when he looks at Carol?

Every day, Mark hoped Camille would come over to visit

Holly, but he didn't see her the rest of the week. In his mind he rehearsed things he could say to her. Polite things. Suave things. Things that would let her know he cared about her and wanted to get to know her better.

Sunday at the park, he was with the band in the bandstand playing a Strauss waltz when Mark saw Camille. She wore a ruffled dress the color of a robin's egg, with a wide-brimmed matching hat draped in the softest gauzy veil. She carried a ruffled parasol, which she twirled carelessly as she strolled along between her parents. Mr. and Mrs. Wilmot were stylishly dressed and appeared to be well off.

Mark could only glance over periodically, then look back at Mr. Klawinski. But once when he happened to glance in Camille's direction, he was sure she winked at him. It was all he could do to keep his mind on his music. How he hoped Jens hadn't seen her yet. Maybe when the band took a break, Mark could get to her first. Surely this time he'd be able to talk.

But Jens had seen her. As soon as Mr. Klawinski indicated they would stop for a half-hour break, Jens moved like greased lightning and was by Camille's side. He held his cap under his arm just as a military officer might do, and he was already introducing himself to Camille's parents. By the time Mark came up, Jens was inviting Camille to take a ride with him on the paddleboats. Harvey was on Mark's heels.

"Oh, yes," Jens said, turning to Mark and Harvey. "These are two friends of mine, Mark Morgan and Harvey Newmire. Boys, these are Mr. and Mrs. Wilmot."

The adults started talking with Harvey and Mark as Jens escorted Camille off to the paddleboats. Over her shoulder Camille looked back and smiled at Mark. At least he thought she was smiling at him. Since Mark had absolutely nothing to say to Mr. and Mrs. Wilmot, he politely, but quickly excused himself.

76

He walked down one of the winding sidewalks, unsure of which direction he should take.

"Wanna go try the ring toss?" Harvey asked, tagging after him.

"Not today." In times past, the three of them would play games in the park. The ring toss was their favorite. They could buy three tosses for a penny, with prizes like a lucky rabbit's foot on a chain, fancy glass-eyed marbles, and little magnifying glasses. But all of that seemed childish today.

"Maybe we could go see Mr. Cramer and his pet seals. They can do some keen tricks," Harvey suggested.

"I've seen the seals. Lots of times." What Mark really wanted to do was go see if Camille would rather be with him than with Jens. What he really didn't want to do was walk around Central Park with Harvey Newmire. He only tolerated Harvey because of Jens. And now Jens had deserted him.

"I'm going back to the bandstand," Mark announced.

"But we have almost forty-five minutes left."

"I know." And with that Mark turned around, went back to the bandstand area, sat down on a park bench, and stayed there for the remainder of the break. He saw Edward and Carol strolling across a grassy area arm in arm. The other members of his family were sitting on a blanket in the shade, drinking cups of lemonade. Mark could go over and be with them, but he didn't much feel like talking to anyone.

How does one go about getting a girl anyway? he wondered. Perhaps he should ask Edward. Or Uncle Abe. He must be doing something wrong. But what? It was a completely new problem to him. A rather strange and bewildering problem. But he was much too embarrassed to ever ask for anyone's advice. Not even Uncle Abe.

As the warm, slow, lazy summer days moved along, Holly and

Camille became close friends. Mark took every possible opportunity to talk to Camille, but it didn't get him far. Either the girls were busy talking and giggling together, or they were on their way out the door to go to Camille's house, or Mark would completely fall all over himself and be unable to say a word. Some nights he scrolled Camille's name over and over in his journal.

Mama kept at Mark to ask Mr. Klawinski about the benefit program for the orphanage. Mark told her he just forgot. Sometimes that was true. After all, it was an easy thing to forget. One time he told her that Mr. Klawinski was too busy for Mark to talk to him privately. "When I leave rehearsals," he said, "Mr. Klawinski is still working with other band members on their parts." But he knew he couldn't put Mama off forever. Still he cringed at the idea.

One quiet Saturday afternoon, Jens telephoned for Mark to come over to his place and see the newest article he'd come across about Mr. Sousa. "One of our customers brought it in for me," he told Mark over the telephone. "Wait'll you see. It's our best one yet. It tells about how he came to write the 'Stars and Stripes Forever.' "

Mark didn't need to hear anything more. Within minutes he had told Mama where he was going and hurried on his way to Kubek's Butcher Shop.

When he arrived, Dirk was wrapping meat orders and Mr. and Mrs. Kubek were waiting on customers. Dirk barely looked up as Mark went by, but he said, "Jens is supposed to be down here working. Now that you're here, we'll probably not get any more work out of him the rest of the day."

Since Mark wasn't sure how to answer, he just scurried by and went up the stairs. He wondered why Dirk was always out of sorts. It must be awful to live with someone so grouchy.

Jens met him in the kitchen. The two-page article was spread out on the table. Together the boys sat down and read every word. Jens was right. It was the best article they had to date. The photograph showed the black-bearded March King in his uniform, complete with flowing cape and baton. And of course the famous white kid gloves. Mr. Sousa wore a new pair of kid gloves for nearly every performance.

From the article they learned that, in 1896, the composer had been traveling from Europe to America after learning about the death of his band manager back in the States.

"He was on the ship when the song came to him," Jens explained. "Listen to this":

> *Suddenly, I began to sense the rhythmic beat of a band playing within my brain. It kept on ceaselessly, playing, playing, playing. Throughout the whole tense voyage, that imaginary band continued to unfold the same themes, echoing and re-echoing the most distinct melody. . . . When we reached shore, I set down the measures that my brain had been play-ing for me, and not a note of it has ever changed.*

Jens and Mark stared at one another, trying to imagine what it would be like to have written such a powerful and stir-ring piece of music—a song that caused audiences to stand to their feet every time it was played.

"Listen to this," Jens went on. "When someone asked him who influenced the famous march, he answered, 'God—and I say this with all reverence.' "

"God," Mark whispered. He remembered what Pastor had said about music being a gift from God. Evidently Mr. Sousa agreed.

Jens read on about Mr. Sousa's memories as a child of hearing military bands at the end of the Civil War and how those memories affected his love for marches and for pageantry and patriotism.

As the two of them talked, Mark felt for a moment as though he and Jens were back like they used to be. Just like their friendship had been before the trip to San Francisco. Before Harvey Newmire. And yes, even before Camille Wilmot. But it was too good to last.

Jens's mama called from the stairwell. "Is a telephone call for you, Mark. Is your uncle Abraham."

"Uncle Abe?" Mark stood up from the table. "What could he want? Coming, Mrs. Kubek. Thank you."

He hurried downstairs with Jens on his heels. Going to the wall phone in the back of the store, Mark picked up the dangling receiver.

"Hello, Uncle Abe. Is something wrong?"

"Hey, Mark. Nothing's wrong. Everything's right! You'll never guess. Charles Hamilton, the famous aeronaut, will be flying his aerodrome over the city this afternoon. I'm stopping by to pick up Holly, and I'll be there to get you and your friend Jens in just a few minutes. We'll drive to the outskirts of town where we can get the best view."

"Wow!" Mark exclaimed. "That's wonderful news, Uncle Abe. But I'm not sure if Jens can go. Would you talk to his papa?"

"Why sure. Put him on the line."

"Mr. Kubek," Mark said, "my uncle would like to talk to you for a moment."

While Mr. Kubek and Uncle Abe were talking, Mark whispered the details to Jens. His friend's eyes grew wide. "Charles Hamilton? Here? I can't believe it."

They'd read about the man named Roy Knabenshue who designed lighter-than-air dirigibles. But it was Hamilton, the daredevil pilot, who flew Knabenshue's airships. Charles Hamilton was the adventurer.

In a moment, Mr. Kubek was off the phone. "You may go," he said. But there was reluctance in his voice. "I know nothing about such strange things as airships, but I can trust my banker, Mr. Stevenson."

"I knew we'd never get any more work out of Jens today," Dirk grumbled.

"Come on," Jens said to Mark. "Let's wait out front."

As they sat on the curb together, Mark thought what a stroke of luck this was. First the article they could share together, and now he and Jens would see the airship together. And no Harvey around!

They had waited only a few minutes when the Oldsmobile came chugging around the corner. Maureen was up front with her father, but in the back sat Holly—and beside her sat Camille. Jens made no bones about rushing right up and jumping in beside Camille almost before the automobile had stopped.

Maureen scooted over in the front seat and said, "Come on up here, Mark. There's plenty of room."

CHAPTER 10

The Warning

The wind rushing past Mark's ears as they drove out of town was not enough to drown out Jens's lively conversation with Camille in the back seat.

"Charles Hamilton is the greatest aeronaut in the country," Mark heard Jens say.

"Even greater than the Wright brothers?" Camille asked.

"Oh yeah. Much greater than either one of them. The Wright brothers are tame as kittens compared to Hamilton."

"Tell me more," Camille pleaded.

"Well, he's told the story many times how when he was in high school, he jumped out of the second-story window of the school building, holding an umbrella to break his fall."

Camille giggled. Then Holly giggled. Mark wondered what was funny.

"Go on," Camille urged. "What else?"

"Hamilton's not afraid of anything. By the time he was eighteen, he was going up in hot air balloons and making parachute jumps as a circus stunt."

"How old is he now?" Uncle Abe wanted to know.

"Twenty-one," Jens answered back.

"So young," Uncle Abe said. "This is an interesting generation coming on."

Jens talked nonstop the entire way out into the country. Mark wished he could say something to make Camille pay attention to him, but he could think of nothing.

Other cars and many carriages were parked along the roadway, where green fields spread out in either direction. Word had it that the aerodrome would pass over at about three-thirty, and many excited townsfolk had come to watch the spectacle. Uncle Abe had his binoculars in hand so they could get a better look.

Camille wanted to get out and walk out in the field. Holly followed close behind, swinging her parasol in the same manner as Camille. Jens jumped out and joined them.

Just then, someone shouted, "There it is!" Shouts went up as all the onlookers gazed toward the east, where people were pointing.

All Mark could make out was a little dot near the horizon, but the dot continued to grow larger. Uncle Abe handed him the binoculars, and then he could see the details. The airship was a hot air balloon with a bullet-shaped contraption hanging beneath where the pilot was riding. On the front was a propeller, and in the back was a rudder.

"How does it move forward?" Mark asked Uncle Abe.

"A gasoline motor runs the propeller, which pushes the air past the ship. The rudder in the back is used to guide the direction of the ship."

"Oh look," Camille squealed. "The pilot's waving." She pulled out her kerchief and waved it. Holly did the same. Jens was jumping up and down and whooping, which made Camille giggle even more.

By now the aerodrome was right over their heads. Mark could only stare with his mouth gaping open. It seemed impossible that a man could actually be flying through the sky as unencumbered as a bird. They passed the binoculars around so each person could have a good look. Seeing the large crowd, pilot Hamilton turned the rudder to maneuver around in a sweeping circle and give the onlookers a long-lasting view of this amazing spectacle.

After that, he continued on toward the west slowly, slowly until the airship once again became a tiny dot on the horizon. Then it vanished from sight.

"Mark, my boy," said Uncle Abe, "I guess you'd better drive us back into town."

"Oh, Mark," Camille said, "you can drive an automobile?"

"I've been driving for a long time," Mark assured her. And his voice didn't crack.

"May I sit up front and watch you drive?" she asked. "May I, Mr. Stevenson?"

Uncle Abe looked at Mark and smiled. "I guess that'll be all right."

"And I get to sit in front, too," Holly added quickly.

A disgruntled Jens crawled into the back seat with Maureen and Uncle Abe, and Mark carefully drove the Oldsmobile back to town. When Jens was dropped off in front of the butcher shop, he mumbled a thank-you to Uncle Abe, then went inside without so much as a smile or a wave.

Mark drove on to Vine Place feeling like a million dollars with the pretty Camille sitting right by his side. She asked him questions about the gears and how the car operated, and he answered every question.

That night he wrote every detail of the wonderful day in his journal. Even to the sweet aroma of Camille's rose water as she sat close by his side.

The next week before Mark left for rehearsal, Mama stopped him in the front hall. "Mark, I'm reminding you to please ask Mr. Klawinski about the benefit concert for the orphanage, because if you don't," she said with a smile, "I'll have to come with you this evening and ask myself."

Mama come to rehearsal? He'd be the laughingstock of all the junior members. "All right, Mama. I'll ask."

"You won't forget?"

"I won't forget."

All the way to rehearsal, Mark wondered how he could ask Mr. Klawinski without Jens or Harvey overhearing. But there seemed to be no way. When he met up with Harvey and Jens at the butcher shop, Jens was still out of sorts from the previous Saturday and he didn't talk much. When the three of them arrived at the rehearsal hall, many of the members were already tuning up. Mark knew he'd have to get it over with as quickly as possible.

Walking right up to Mr. Klawinski, he said, "Sir, my mama and my aunt volunteer their services at the rescue mission and the orphanage over on skid row."

Mr. Klawinski looked up from his music stand. "Yes? The orphanage?"

"Yes, sir. The orphanage, and the mission as well. They volunteer there. And they wondered if you would consider talking to them about holding a benefit concert."

"Hmm. A benefit concert?" He tapped the baton against his hand. "I don't believe we've ever done such a thing, but I like the sound of it. Where would this take place?"

Mark swallowed hard, hoping Jens wasn't within earshot. "At the mission. They hope to draw the city's attention to the work there."

Mr. Klawinski nodded. "Sounds like a splendid idea. Tell them to give me a call."

"Thank you, sir. I'll tell Mama."

When Mark went to his place and opened his case, Jens and Harvey came over to him and reacted just as Mark expected.

"Your mama wants the brass band to play at the *mission*?" Jens asked. "Who'd want to play in an awful place like that?"

"Yeah," Harvey added. "The rescue mission is a long way from the bandstand at Central Park. In more ways than one."

Mark didn't defend himself. He'd done what he'd been asked to do and that was that.

During practice that evening, Mr. Klawinski looked troubled as he listened to the clarinets playing one part by themselves. He cocked his head and listened, then squinted his eyes and listened some more. He asked Jens and Harvey to play the part alone.

Mark knew they'd been listening to the ragtime music so much they were beginning to mimic the style. That's what Mr. Klawinski was hearing. Mark wondered if their conductor could hear it in Mark's playing as well. Was the music changing his style? He'd never stopped feeling guilty for listening to the music, even though he had to admit he liked the rhythm and the beat. And he also had to admit he enjoyed practicing at Harvey's house. They were never bothered or interrupted.

Sure enough, Mr. Klawinski asked the three of them to remain after rehearsal. When the room was empty of all the other players, he gently but firmly reminded them that they were a part of a larger group.

"I didn't ask you to come onboard to be soloists or even individual stylists," he said. "There'll be plenty of time for that later in your lives. For now, please attend to basics. Learn the basics first. Is that clear?"

They all answered in the affirmative. As they walked down the sidewalk from the drugstore to the butcher shop, Jens mumbled his displeasure at being reprimanded. Harvey agreed.

"I guess we can play anything we like," Harvey said, "even if we are in his band. After all, he chose us over a lot of other kids."

Mark said nothing, but in his heart he knew Mr. Klawinski was right. Had his own style changed that much? How he wished he had an objective ear and could know for certain.

When he arrived home, he told Mama about Mr. Klawinski's positive reaction to the idea of a benefit concert. "Wait till Elise hears this," she said. Seeing Mama so happy made Mark pleased that he'd done as she asked.

As the heat of late July pressed in, the Morgan house was astir with plans for Carol's wedding. Mark was never sure if Carol's face was flushed from heat or from joy. She laughed a lot, and Edward was always at the house. Now it wasn't only Mark's noise that bothered Christopher.

The novel was giving Christopher so many problems that he decided to take on a few article assignments. He had to be away from the house to get the stories. Mark was almost ashamed to admit it, but he was relieved to have his stepfather gone for a while.

One afternoon when Mark was at the house, Mama received a strange phone call. Carol, Allyson, and Mama were in the kitchen discussing details of the wedding dinner with Stella. Mama was on the telephone when Mark walked in to find something cold to drink from the icebox. As he pulled out the pitcher of lemonade, Mama turned from the phone ashen-faced. "That was Mrs. Detwiler."

"Mrs. Detwiler?" Carol said. "From over on the next block?" Mama nodded.

"What'd she want?" Allyson asked. She stepped to Mama's side because she could see Mama was very upset.

"She says Holly and another girl were on their roller skates and they ran her off the sidewalk."

Stella shook her head. "Not our Holly. She must have been mistaken."

"No. No mistake." Mama took a breath and smoothed her hair, tucking a strand into her chignon in back. "It was Holly and a friend. A friend with curly hair."

"That girl named Camille," Allyson said.

Mark filled his glass with lemonade and set the pitcher back in the icebox.

Carol pulled out a chair and helped Mama to sit down. "What else did Mrs. Detwiler say?"

"She said the girls just laughed."

"Laughed?" Carol was incredulous. "That doesn't sound like Holly at all."

As Mark left the room, Allyson was asking Mama what she was going to do about the matter. Mark didn't want to hear the answer. He went to his room and practiced his trumpet for a full hour until he heard Christopher returning.

CHAPTER 11
Holly Rebels

Holly had talked back to Mama! Mark could hardly believe it. He would never have known about it, but he accidentally heard Allyson and Carol discussing the matter. Mama had reprimanded Holly, and Holly had snipped back that she had as much right to the sidewalk as that old biddy, Mrs. Detwiler.

In his journal, Mark wrote:

Dear Michael,
Holly has treated Mama with disrespect. I can't understand why she would do such a thing. I feel all achy inside for Mama. None of us kids has ever talked back to her before. What's happening to Holly? I can't figure it out.

After being reprimanded by Mr. Klawinski, Mark determined to practice at home every day. The music they performed with the brass band was more demanding than anything Mark had ever attempted. One afternoon when Mama and the girls had gone shopping, Mark began practice by repeatedly going over the trouble spots until he had perfected them. Suddenly there was a tap on the door. It was Christopher.

"Mark," he said, "I know you need to practice, but can you do it somewhere else? I thought you had a friend's place where you could go." Christopher's eyes were bloodshot, and his hair looked like it had never been combed that day. "I'm so near done. But the last few chapters are giving me fits. I'm struggling to finish by the deadline. I must make that deadline, Mark. Can you understand that?"

After Christopher went back to his office, Mark telephoned Harvey. That afternoon as they practiced, Mark joined in some of the ragtime improvisations that Jens and Harvey enjoyed doing. Joining them was much easier than going against them. And it was fun!

The next week brought more phone calls from Fair Oaks neighbors. Holly and Camille were caught teasing a kitten belonging to one of the neighborhood children. One afternoon they were rolling metal hoops and went through someone's flower beds. Mama seemed to be at a loss to know what to do.

One Sunday morning as they were eating breakfast, Holly came to the table dressed in one of her cotton play dresses. Everyone at the table stared in disbelief. Even Christopher looked at his stepdaughter with wide eyes.

"Holly Morgan," Mama said sternly. "What is the meaning of this? Go back upstairs and change into your church clothes this instant."

Holly sat down and helped herself to the scrambled eggs. "I'm staying home from church."

Mark felt his stomach tighten in a hard ball. What had come over his sister? Had she lost her mind? She calmly buttered a biscuit and began to eat her eggs.

Christopher said, "Holly, did you hear your mother? Go change for church."

Holly looked him square in the eyes. "You stay home sometimes. Why can't I?"

"Holly!" Mama said in a shocked tone. "Christopher has been working hard on his novel. That's the only reason he would ever stay home from church."

"So, he has his reasons, and I have mine. Who's to say his are better than mine? Besides, Camille and her family never go to church, and she's a nice girl."

"What's Camille got to do with this?" Carol asked. But Mama looked at Carol and shook her head. Mama would handle this. Mama stood up, went to Holly's place, and removed her plate.

"No breakfast for you just yet, young lady. You're coming upstairs with me. And if you're not in your church clothes inside of ten minutes, I'll dress you myself. Don't think for a moment I can't do it."

Holly pushed back her chair and sullenly went upstairs with Mama.

Holly did go to church that day, but she wasn't allowed to play outside for the next three days. Nor was she allowed to go to the orphanage to help Mama volunteer. She told Mark she didn't care about the old orphanage anyway.

But Mark knew it was terrible to have to stay inside on such beautiful summer days. Especially when it was cool under the shade trees and in the grass and very hot in the house. When

Camille came to visit Holly, Mama told her Holly was busy and couldn't come out and play.

One time when Camille came, Mark was there. After she left, Mark hurried out the back door and came around to meet her down the street. As he came close to her, he caught a whiff of sweet rose water. "Since Holly can't come out, may I walk you home?" he asked.

"Why I suppose so," she said and then gave a little giggle. "Since Jens isn't here to push you out of the way."

Mark fell into step with her. "Jens doesn't push me out of the way," he countered, wondering what she meant.

"Sure he does. That is, whenever you let him." She smiled and her dimples flashed.

Mark felt his throat closing tight. "I guess that's true," he said, and his voice cracked.

Camille laughed again and it sounded like a rippling brook rushing over smooth stones. "Your parents are very strict, aren't they?"

"Why do you say that?" Mark didn't think they were strict at all.

"Holly told me. She says she never has any fun. And when we tried to have fun, she got into trouble."

"Mama has never allowed us to disobey her or talk back. But she's very fair with us." Mark felt he had to defend Mama.

"But she forces you to go to church. Holly says it's dull and boring."

Mark thought about that. It had never occurred to him to question whether church service was boring or not. They went and that was that. He rather liked church service, especially the music.

Changing the subject, Camille asked, "Do you like ragtime music?"

"I sure do. Listen to it all the time." He was careful not to mention that he wasn't allowed to do so at home.

"I have some records. Would you like to listen to some of them on our gramophone?"

"I sure would."

"Come on." She grabbed his hand. "I'll see if the cook will fix us something cold to drink."

Mark was certain he'd never wash his hand again—ever.

Camille's mother was polite, but rather cool and distant. When she looked at Mark, he felt that he didn't quite measure up to what she expected Camille's friends to be like. Camille seemed to sense her mother's feelings as well. When Mrs. Wilmot had left the room, she said, "Pay no mind to Mother. It takes her a while to warm up to people."

They sat on the sofa in the parlor, listened to ragtime music, and ate big sugar cookies with colored sprinkles on top. Later, when it was time to go, Camille walked Mark to the door. As he went out, she said. "Come back anytime. You're a lot more fun than your sister." Then she winked and giggled.

Michael was the only one Mark confided to about his time spent at Camille's house that afternoon. It was a wonderful secret all his own. He was sure that Camille really liked him. Wouldn't Jens be surprised.

At the next rehearsal, Harvey, Jens, and Mark were once again asked to stay behind. This time it was much more serious.

"Boys," Mr. Klawinski began, "I've tried to explain how necessary it is for each of you to have the same sound as all the rest of the band, but my warnings seem to be falling on deaf ears. I would have been more than willing to work with any one of you privately, but you never cared enough to seek out my assistance. It seems you'd rather try to learn on your own. But what you are learning is harming our entire band."

He pulled out his handkerchief and mopped his glistening forehead. The upstairs room was stifling hot. "Whatever you want to listen to is up to you. But how it affects the band is up to me. You are hereby dismissed from the Municipal Brass Band. You will turn your uniforms in as soon as possible."

Mark grabbed his trumpet case and ran out the door and down the stairs. He didn't stop running until he got home. Then he made sure no one saw him as he crept upstairs, fell across his bed, and cried like a little baby.

CHAPTER 12

A Second Chance

The family was shocked to learn of Mark's dismissal. Since he refused to talk about it, they assumed the music had become too difficult for him to handle. On the following Sunday, he begged Mama to let him stay home from the park. She was kind and said he could. He was too ashamed to talk to anyone. He especially couldn't bear to face Camille. What would she think of him?

Late that afternoon, Mark was all alone in the house. He wandered from room to room as though he were lost. Throughout the house were signs of the upcoming wedding—a wedding that had nothing to do with him. The only good thing about it was that Peter would be home to take part.

Anger and shame washed over Mark as he thought of his misfortune. He was even angry at Christopher for having forced him back to Harvey's house. How would he ever face the other band members again? Just as he had decided to go upstairs and write in his journal, the knocker sounded at the front door. It was Uncle Abe.

"Hey there, sport. Sure missed you at the concert."

Mark looked around his uncle to see who else was with him. No one was there. The automobile wasn't even there. He'd walked over from the park.

"Would you like to talk?" Uncle Abe asked.

Mark shrugged. "I suppose."

"How about the sunporch. It ought to be cooler out there." Mark's tall, lanky uncle led the way down the hall toward the back of the house. "Stella have the afternoon off?"

"Yes, sir." Mark couldn't figure out for the life of him why Uncle Abe was here.

Once he was settled into the chaise, Uncle Abe said, "Your mama tells me you've been released from the band. Don't tell me they promoted you to Sousa's group and you're leaving town."

Mark tried to laugh at the humor.

"What happened, Mark?" Uncle Abe said, growing serious. "You loved being in that band."

Mark hoped against hope that the hot tears in his eyes would stay put. At first he stammered. But then the truth came out in a torrent. "I never realized what I listened to could affect my style that much—but Mr. Klawinski has a keen ear and can hear every shade of variation."

"So why didn't you do as he said after the first warning?"

"I tried. I made up my mind to never practice at Harvey's house again. But Christopher needs it quiet, and he asked me not to practice here anymore."

Uncle Abe shook his head. "Let me ask you something, Mark. If you had a special place to practice, would you stop listening to the ragtime music?"

Mark shrugged. "It wouldn't help the situation. I'm out of the band for good."

"Don't be too hasty. If you explained to Mr. Klawinski the problems you've had with being able to practice, perhaps he would give you a second chance."

Mark looked at Uncle Abe. "What are you thinking?"

"No one's living above our carriage house this summer. What if that became your place to practice your trumpet?"

"Uncle Abe, do you really mean it? Could I?"

"Why, of course. In fact if you'd stated your problem sooner, we could have solved it sooner. That's why the Bible says we have not because we ask not."

"Mr. Klawinski said almost the same thing. That we could have come to him and he would have worked with us, if we'd only asked."

"All right. That's settled. I'll telephone Mr. Klawinski and ask him to meet with you and me in my office at the bank."

"Would you? Honest?"

"I'll do it first thing tomorrow morning. But then you'll have to keep your part of the deal—strict discipline in your practice."

"I'll do anything." Mark paused. "But what about Jens and Harvey?"

"I'm afraid you can't fix their problem, Mark. At this moment you have your hands full working out your own solutions."

Mark nodded. "One more thing," he said.

"What's that?"

"Please don't tell Mama about the ragtime music."

"You have my word."

Mr. Klawinski was kind and understanding. Much more understanding than Mark had any right to deserve. The conductor thanked Uncle Abe kindly for explaining the situation about Christopher.

"I've never written a novel," he told them, "but when I'm working on arranging orchestral pieces, I must have absolute quiet. So I can understand your stepfather's predicament. I'd let you work in the rehearsal hall, but we've promised Mr. Rose no one would ever practice there except during scheduled rehearsals. Otherwise, he'd have to do the same thing your stepfather did."

So it was settled. Mark told neither Harvey nor Jens that he had his uniform back. When they invited him to Harvey's house, he told them he'd decided not to listen to the ragtime music anymore. Mark began to lengthen his practice to two hours a day rather than the one. Within the first week, he could detect definite improvements. At rehearsal, Mr. Klawinski was all smiles.

Mark wondered what he would tell Jens and Harvey when he showed up at the bandstand on Sunday in uniform. But as it turned out, he didn't have to. Neither of them was there. They were probably in Harvey's basement improvising more wild ragtime melodies.

Camille, however, was there. She and Holly were sitting together on a quilt under a shade tree. Camille's soft pink dress was spread out around her like rose petals. Mark tried not to look in her direction, because when he did, she would smile and wink, making it difficult for him to concentrate.

During a break in the music, Camille came hurrying toward

him. "Oh, Mark, your playing is simply splendid."

"How can you tell when all the sounds are blended?"

"I just know, that's all."

"Camille," Holly said, "where're you going?"

Over her shoulder Camille said, "Mark and I are taking a walk." Turning to him, she said, "Aren't we?"

"Well, yes. I guess we are." But Mark noticed the disappointed look on his sister's face. He wondered if she felt the same way he did when Jens started befriending Harvey.

As they walked down the gravel path toward the lake, Camille asked Mark if he would come to her house one afternoon next week to listen to records.

Mark hesitated. How he wanted another afternoon like the two of them had spent before, laughing and talking about the music. Yet he'd promised Uncle Abe, and he'd promised Mr. Klawinski.

"What's the matter?" Camille asked, making her pretty mouth into a little pout. "You don't want to come and be with me?"

"Oh, it's not that. Truly, Camille, I like being with you very much. But I've learned that listening to the wrong music causes me to play differently than the band."

"So what? Why do you need to be like all of them? Shouldn't you be free to express yourself in your own way?"

Mark wasn't sure how to explain it. "Mr. Klawinski says it's important to learn the basics first because I'm just beginning to formulate my style."

"How narrow-minded." Her voice was a little cooler.

"But I'd be pleased to come over and maybe just talk. Or do something else together."

"Never mind. I happen to like the new exciting music. Maybe I'll just wait until I can find someone who likes the same things I do." She turned and started to walk away. "I

99

guess I'll be getting on back. I think Holly wanted me to go do something with her."

She was gone. Mark whipped off his hat and hit his leg with it hard. "Confound it, anyhow!" he muttered. "Why does everything have to be so complicated?"

Uncle Abe's spacious, grassy backyard was filled with noisy, laughing young people. Some were playing lawn tennis, others were involved in a lively game of croquet. Uncle Abe and Aunt Elise enjoyed throwing parties for Maureen and her friends. A number of them were Maureen's age, others were girls from Holly's class.

Jens and Harvey had been invited as well. They now knew that Mark had been reinstated into the band. As could be expected, it caused hard feelings. Uncle Abe encouraged Mark to be kind, but not apologetic.

"They could make the same commitment you made," Uncle Abe told Mark. "After all, Harvey has a quiet place to practice."

Mark knew that was true, but it was still difficult.

Camille spent the warm afternoon flitting from one young man to another like a pretty little butterfly going from flower to flower. It made Mark ache inside to watch her.

"Hey there, Mark," Aunt Elise called to him. "If you're not involved in a game just now, would you go inside and help Maureen bring out more refreshments."

"Sure."

In the kitchen, Maureen was putting cookies and slices of cake out on a tray.

"Excuse me, Maureen."

His voice startled her. "Mark, I didn't even hear you come in."

"Aunt Elise sent me to help. What needs to be done?"

She looked about the room. "I'm not sure. I guess you could get the melon from the icebox. We'll cut it in slices," she said, then returned to her work.

Mark looked at his cousin. Suddenly it dawned on him that, like him, she had been sitting out the games all afternoon.

Bending down in front of the icebox, he flipped open the handle and pulled the cold watermelon out. "You're awfully quiet," he said, not looking at her. "Is anything wrong?"

"Not really."

"Where's the butcher knife?"

She pointed to a drawer. "In there."

Mark glanced over at Maureen. She was wiping a tear off her cheek. He stepped over to her. "I thought so. There *is* something wrong."

She answered with a little sniffle, pulled a handkerchief from her dress pocket, and wiped away the tears.

"Maybe you should try writing it in a journal," he said, making a stab at a joke. "Then you don't have to carry the thoughts around with you. I hear it works well."

She looked up at him and smiled through her glistening tears. He was surprised to realize he was a few inches taller than she was. Mama had said he'd already grown about a foot that summer. Maybe she hadn't been exaggerating.

"We used to tell one another most everything, didn't we?" he said. "I wonder what happened to that?"

She shrugged. "Time, I guess. Time and circumstances."

"But we could go back just for this afternoon. Is it something you can't tell Aunt Elise?"

She shook her head. "Oh, Mark, it's really so piddly. I'm ashamed to even talk about it."

"But not to me."

"If you must know, it's about Holly."

"Holly?" In a way, Mark wasn't surprised. They'd all been concerned about Holly.

"There for a while, I felt like her older sister. At times, closer than a sister. Especially when I was teaching her all about our work at the orphanage. Then—after Camille came along—she changed."

Mark felt himself tense. He didn't want to hear Camille spoken about in this way. Yet he had asked Maureen to tell him.

"Now Holly mocks the children there and acts as though she's better than they are and sometimes even acts as though she's better than I am. One day she reminded me that I'd been the child of Mama's cook."

Mark could hardly believe Holly would say such a cruel thing. They all knew Uncle Abe and Aunt Elise had adopted Maureen after her mother died.

"What did you say?" Mark asked.

"I told her she needn't remind me, because Mother and Father and I discuss it quite often. I told her I had nothing to hide."

"What else?"

"She never talks to me anymore. It's not as though I don't have other friends. You know I do."

Mark nodded. It was true. Nearly every student in Maureen's class liked her.

"But I can't get rid of the sense of loss. Almost as though I'd lost my very own little sister."

Mark suddenly felt a stab of guilt. He'd been so immersed in his own problems, he'd practically ignored Holly's. It never occurred to him that he should be concerned. Now it appeared Maureen was more concerned than he was.

Again she dabbed at her eyes and blew her nose. "I'm sorry,

Mark. I know I'm being such a baby about all this."

"I don't think caring about someone makes you a baby."

"Thank you. You're so understanding."

"You know, Maureen. When Father was alive and we came to him with problems, he always wanted to pray about it. Maybe we should do that now."

"I think you're right."

Mark gently took his cousin's hand, and they both offered a simple prayer for Holly. Afterward Mark felt much better. As he cut the watermelon and placed the slices in the large bowls Maureen gave him, he thought about how confused he'd been in his friendship with Jens. Somehow it helped to know someone else had a similar problem.

CHAPTER 13

Trouble at School

Mark was convinced: There was nothing like a wedding to make a guy feel totally useless. And as if all the fuss wasn't enough, Peter added to the confusion by bringing a guest home with him from the university.

Mama had sweetly said, "Yes, of course," when Peter first telephoned to ask. But Mark could see the strain on her face. There was already so much to do.

The surprise came when they drove to the station to meet Peter. The guest was a girl! Mark felt his stomach drop to his toes. Peter had promised him the two of them would do something together the next time he came home. Mark knew it was now out of the question. He could tell by the way Peter looked at this girl that there would be no pulling him away from her.

The girl's name was Louise, and the whole family took to her immediately. Her travel trunks were taken to Allyson's room. She would stay there until Carol moved out following the wedding. Then she would stay in Carol's room for the remainder of her visit.

On Carol and Edward's wedding day, it must have been one hundred degrees in the shade. Everyone was dripping from perspiration, especially Christopher, who was more nervous than on his own wedding day. The only thing that kept Mark from feeling completely left out was when he looked at Maureen and remembered their talk. He watched how Holly treated Maureen. His cousin was right. Holly ignored Maureen completely.

The church was packed with guests, most of whom were fanning themselves with the cardboard fans kept in the hymnal racks. Mark and a cousin of Edward's helped seat the guests. When the organ pumped out the first strains of the "Wedding March," Mark took his seat near the front beside Mama.

As Christopher walked down the aisle with Carol on his arm, Mama was softly weeping. Mark knew she was probably wishing Father could see his daughter in all her beauty. And Mark had to agree, Carol was indeed very beautiful. Even Peter, who was standing up with Edward, was teary-eyed. In a few minutes the happy couple kissed, and it was all over. Mark had to stand and let the guests leave one row at a time. That gave the couple time to get to the church basement, where the reception was held.

Later that evening, Mama held a large dinner at the house for many of the out-of-town guests. When dinner was nearly over and many toasts had been made to the happy couple,

Christopher stood to make an announcement.

When everyone was quiet, he said, "My novel is completed and has been mailed." The guests applauded and cheered, but no one showed more enthusiasm than the members of Mark's family.

"The good news is, my editors like it very much and it will be out next spring." Again there was applause. "Thank you," Christopher said, smiling broadly. "The next part of my news is that I've presented an idea for a second novel, and it's been accepted as well."

Mark looked at Allyson, and they both rolled their eyes. Mark guessed they'd have to face it—Christopher was an author and he would be writing books for a long time to come.

Their stepfather went on to thank his wife and children for their patience with him over the past few months of grueling work. "They say the first book is the most difficult, so I expect it to be a little easier from here on out. No man has ever had a better family nor been less deserving of them." Lifting his water glass, he said, "Here, here! A toast to my wife and my children."

"Here, here!" echoed all the guests, joining in the toast.

Mark sighed. He was anxious to have all this folderol done with. He was thinking of tomorrow at the park when Peter would have a chance to see him in uniform for the first time. He could hardly wait to hear Peter's reaction.

The next evening, Mark wasn't disappointed. Peter and Louise chose a park bench close to the bandstand and stayed there throughout the concert. When the first break came, Peter shook Mark's hand and said, "I'm so proud of you, I'm about to bust right out of my coat buttons."

Louise was also especially impressed that Mark was part of such a "prestigious group," as she called the brass band.

Those words made all the practice and all the sacrifices

worth it—even the sacrifice of not getting to spend time with Camille.

With the end of summer came the end of the junior band members' time with the brass band. Mark dreaded the day he would have to turn in his uniform. Through the course of the season, he felt he'd earned it.

At the final rehearsal for junior members, Mr. Klawinski bade good-bye, thanked each junior member, and shook their hands. But when Mark came up, he said, "Mark, could you stay back for a few minutes? I'd like a word with you."

"All right, sir." Mark went off to the side to sit down until the room had emptied.

Then Mr. Klawinski pulled up another folding chair and sat down beside him.

"I guess your mama has told you we're playing the benefit for the orphanage just before Christmas."

"Actually, sir, there's been a wedding at our house. Mama's mind hasn't exactly been on Christmas, so I had not heard."

Mr. Klawinski smiled and smoothed his mustache. "I have married daughters," he said. "I understand fully."

Mark still wasn't sure why he'd been asked to stay. It certainly wasn't about his playing abilities this time.

"I want to commend you on all your hard work this summer, Mark. I see a great deal of potential in your abilities."

"Thank you, sir." Mark could think of no greater compliment.

"I kept you behind to invite you to stay with the band through Christmas. We have two more concerts in the park in September, a fall concert at the Municipal Opera House, and of course the benefit in December—which came about because of you."

Mark just sat there for a moment, stunned. Could he be

dreaming? No other junior member had been asked to stay on.

"This means you'll be practicing numbers with us and also numbers with your school band. That's in addition to your regular schoolwork. Think you can handle that kind of challenge?"

"Oh yes, sir! I can do it. Well, at least I'll do my best."

Mr. Klawinski laughed. "That's all I ask. It's settled then. You're with us until Christmas. Then I expect you to be a member again next summer."

"Yes, sir!" Mark stood to go.

"And don't forget your uniform."

Mark had turned in his uniform earlier that evening. Now he went into the storeroom to fetch it. It made the third time it'd been given to him!

"Good-bye, Mr. Klawinski," he said on his way out. "And thank you so much!"

Being part of the oldest class at Fair Oaks Elementary School was a grand experience. Everyone in the eighth-grade class sensed how special it was to be at the top. Next year, they'd again be the youngest, but for now Mark reveled in this experience.

The only bad thing was not having Maureen around. Even though she and Mark had never spent much time together at school, he always saw her between classes. But not this year. It left an empty place in Mark's world. Besides that, Jens would hardly speak to him—that, too, was difficult.

One day, however, Jens came up to Mark and handed him an article. "Here," he said. "You can keep this one. It tells how Mr. Sousa is using ragtime music in his concerts. Evidently he doesn't think it's so bad. So there, Mister Know-it-all." With that he stomped off.

Mark read the article during lunch and wondered about it. Who was right?

Camille made a big splash as the new student. Mark watched as the girls fought to sit by her at lunch. As she sat on the grass beneath the shade tree, she looked like a queen holding court.

There was something about her presence that demanded attention. When she walked into the classroom, every head turned. It was her soft curly hair, her twinkling eyes, her dimples. It was all of that. Mark knew it was more, but he wasn't sure exactly what. How did she hold such sway over people?

In band class that afternoon, Mr. Schoggen commended the band members who'd spent the summer with the brass band. He surprised them by presenting each one with an award. Mark planned to frame his and hang it on his bedroom wall next to the pictures of John Philip Sousa. Since Jens and Harvey had not completed the season, there were no certificates for them.

Their eighth-grade teacher, a tall willowy lady by the name of Miss Gallaway, had read the press notices about Christopher Wilkins's upcoming novel. When she mentioned it in class, Mark blushed . But Jens groaned right out loud. "Not again," Mark heard him mutter.

"To have an author right in our community is a privilege," Miss Gallaway told the class. "But to have his family here in our school is even more of a privilege." She explained to the new students that Mark was the stepson of this noted author. "Mark, do you think your stepfather would come and talk to us about writing?"

Mark had no idea Miss Gallaway planned to do this, or he would have asked her not to say anything. This was much like last year when he'd been asked to talk about San Francisco.

"He's pretty busy," Mark said lamely. Actually he had no idea whether Christopher would want to come to the school or not.

"Perhaps if I wrote a note of invitation. . . But we can discuss it later."

Mark didn't dare look at Jens for fear of what he'd see there. After school, though, Jens cornered him in the cloakroom and said, "First it was your great trip to California, then you wheedled your way back into the brass band and you got a little paper certificate from Mr. Schoggen. But now we have to listen to your *famous* stepfather give a boring talk about writing. What is it with you anyway?" Jens grabbed his clarinet case from the shelf. "You must think you're pretty hot stuff."

Mark tried to think of an answer, but Jens turned and left. Mark guessed there'd be no going over to Jens's house after school this year.

As he tried to slip out of the classroom, Miss Gallaway stopped him. "Mark," she said. "Don't forget the invitation I wrote for your stepfather."

Mark stopped. "No, ma'am." He shoved the note in his pocket and headed out of the building. As he came out, he saw Jens and Harvey walking on either side of Camille. Jens was carrying her books. Mark took the long way around to avoid passing them. Seeing them walking together filled him with loneliness.

CHAPTER 14

The Letter

Mark went straight to Christopher's study when he arrived at the house. He knew if he didn't deliver the note right away, he might not do it at all.

The family members didn't often go into Christopher's study. It was his domain, littered with sheets of papers, wadded-up paper on the floor, open books lying about, and stacks of pages that Mark knew were the completed chapters. No one touched a thing. Mama joked that she and Stella cleaned in there only between novels.

When Mark tapped on the door, he didn't know what Christopher would say. He'd been known to say "Not now" or "Go away." This time, however, Christopher simply asked, "Who's there?"

"Me. Mark. May I talk to you a minute?"

"Sure. Come on in."

Mark entered cautiously.

"It's all right. I can't go any further just now." Christopher waved at the paper in the typewriter. "I'm stuck at this scene. What's on your mind?"

"My teacher has heard about your book." Mark pulled the note out of his pocket. "She's wondering if you'd come talk to our class about writing."

"Talk to your class? Now that's an interesting thought." Christopher reached out to take the note and waved Mark toward the nearby chair. Mark removed a thick dictionary and sat down. After reading the invitation, Christopher said, "She doesn't mention time. Do you know if she had a date in mind?"

Mark shook his head. "No, sir." He held his breath, hoping Christopher would say he was much too busy to do such a thing.

"If there are any writing 'hopefuls' in your class," Christopher said, "a talk from me might be just the thing that would encourage them." Taking his pen from its holder and a sheet of stationery from his drawer, he quickly wrote down his reply.

"I'll make time some afternoon to come and talk," Christopher said as the pen scratched across the page. Folding the paper, he slipped it into an envelope and handed it to Mark. "I'm pleased she cared enough to ask. She sounds like a conscientious teacher."

Mark rose to go. As he did, he caught sight of the corner of an envelope buried under the papers on Christopher's desk. It looked like. . . But it couldn't be.

"Excuse me, Christopher, but that envelope on your desk looks like it has the name of Sousa on it."

Christopher laughed. "I guess it looks that way because it does have his name on it." Pulling the letter from beneath the stack, he held it up for Mark to see.

Mark felt his knees go weak, and he sat back down. "You have a letter from John Philip Sousa?"

"That I do. In fact, I've been going to tell you about this, but I get so involved in the novel, I forget other things. Mr. Sousa is lobbying for copyright laws for composers, artists, and authors so we will receive the monies due us for our work."

Mark stared at the envelope. It was actually written in the March King's handwriting.

"Here," Christopher said, handing it to him. "It won't bite."

Reverently, Mark held the envelope in his hand. "What does a copyright law have to do with?"

"Sousa says that mechanical music will ruin talented composers if they aren't paid royalties for the use of their music."

"You mean gramophones and recordings?"

"And piano rolls. The producers use the music without paying the composers a penny. Mr. Sousa and Victor Herbert are partners in fighting for legislation to change this. They testified at hearings in Washington last summer."

"Do you know him personally? Mr. Sousa?"

Christopher shook his head. "I'm just another name on his vast mailing list. However, I've written him my views because I agree with what they're trying to do."

The address on the letter said, "Sands Point, Long Island." As Mark looked at it, he formed a plan.

"The legislation didn't pass," Christopher went on, "because the lobbies for the recording industry are bigger. But Sousa and Herbert have created an organization for authors and composers. Next time, we hope to win."

Mark nodded and handed back the letter. He was only half listening. He kept thinking of Jens's comments about Mr. Sousa playing ragtime music. Maybe now he could find out the truth. He'd just write a letter and ask. "Thank you," Mark said, standing up. "I'd better go now."

"Don't forget my note to Miss Gallaway."

"Oh yeah." Mark grabbed the note and flew out the door.

By the time he reached his room, Mark had almost talked himself out of writing to Mr. Sousa. It was a far-fetched idea. After all, the March King was always on tour. Not only was he a busy man, but he probably received thousands of letters from his admirers around the world. A letter from Mark would only get buried in the stacks.

Mark sat down at his desk to think. He should be at Uncle Abe's right now for his after-school practice session. He stared out the window at the bright afternoon sunshine streaming through the leafy maples.

From his desk he took a sheet of paper and began writing:

Dear Mr. Sousa,

I got your address from my stepfather, author Christopher Wilkins. I hope you don't mind me writing to you, but I have an important question.

My mother doesn't allow me to listen to ragtime music, and my conductor of the Municipal Brass Band (I was a junior member last summer) says it will ruin my style if I listen to it all the time. Yet your band plays ragtime music. Please tell me who is right and who is wrong. I'm very confused.

Yours truly,
Mark Morgan

114

When he had finished, Mark felt better. Folding the letter, he stuffed it into an envelope. He would purchase a stamp at the post office tomorrow. But for now, he had to hurry to Uncle Abe's and get his practicing done before supper.

Meals at home seemed strange without Carol. Mark would have sworn early in the summer that he would never miss Carol. After all, she didn't talk about anything except school. But he'd been wrong. He missed his oldest sister very much. He found himself hoping that Allyson wouldn't meet anyone soon. He wanted her to stay around as long as possible.

This term, Allyson spent her mornings practice teaching and her afternoons in classes. She lamented that Carol wasn't there to hear of her daily experiences and give words of wisdom.

Mama kept saying, "No need to fret. Carol's only a few minutes away from us." But it wasn't the same, and they all knew it.

More and more, Mark poured out his heart on the pages of his journal. He was greatly pleased with his trumpet playing abilities, but so many other things seemed to be a mess.

Holly began to get in trouble with her sixth-grade teacher from the first day of school. By the end of the second week, two notes had come home from the teacher saying that Holly wasn't paying attention, that she talked in class, and that she had been caught passing notes.

"My teacher doesn't like me," Holly said one night at supper. "And I don't like her, either."

Mama replied, "You don't have to like your teacher, Holly. But you must respect her."

"How can I respect someone who's unfair?" she demanded.

"And how is she unfair?" Allyson wanted to know.

"She picks on me. I'm not doing anything that other kids aren't doing."

Mark thought about what Holly had said. Camille also passed notes in class and talked out of turn. When she got in trouble with Miss Gallaway, she made a pouty face and said, "Why do you always pick on me?" Could it be Camille who was having a negative effect on his sister? Was Holly trying to be like her? And if so, what could be done about it?

Mama seemed almost at her wit's end. All the punishment she'd set forth had accomplished little. How Mark wished Father were there.

Then late one evening as Mark was propped up in bed going over the music for the brass band fall concert, a knock sounded at his door.

"Mark?" It was Christopher.

"It's open."

Christopher was in his silk robe and house shoes. "Sorry to bother you, Mark. Could I talk for a minute?"

Mark wondered if he were in trouble. He pointed to the desk chair. "Sure."

Pulling the chair closer to the bed, Christopher sat down. He looked like he couldn't figure out what to say.

"What is it? Is there a problem?"

"You know the problem, Mark. I was wondering if you could help me with the answers. What's happening to Holly? Why is she getting in trouble all of a sudden?"

Why, Mark wondered, *is Christopher asking me?*

"I don't really know," Mark said.

Raking his fingers through his hair, Christopher explained, "This business of being a parent is new to me, Mark. But the rest of you children have made it easy. Your mother is terribly upset, and I feel I should step in and help. But I'm at a loss as to what to do."

Mark couldn't imagine a parent not knowing how to handle

a situation. Perhaps parenting was rather like playing a musical instrument—it required a lot of practice. Christopher had not had much practice.

_"Your uncle Abe was new to parenting when they adopted Maureen, but he seems to have great success with her."

"Uncle Abe spends lots of time with Maureen," Mark said. "He talks to her, he asks her opinions, and he listens to her."

Christopher studied the rug beside Mark's bed. "I don't do that much, do I?"

"No, sir. Not much."

"Not at all, is that right?"

Mark nodded. "That's right."

Christopher stood up slowly, returned the chair to the desk, and stepped toward the door. "Thank you, Mark." And he was gone.

When Christopher came to address the eighth-grade class, Jens and Harvey misbehaved and got in trouble with Miss Gallaway. All the other kids were pleased to have him come. Even Camille appeared to be impressed.

Harvey had always been the class clown, saying and doing silly things just to get attention. Now he and Jens were a team of clowns, and even Mr. Schoggen had given them continual warnings.

On a chilly afternoon late in October, Mark stayed after school to talk to Mr. Schoggen about a piece of music. When Mark was about to leave, Mr. Schoggen said, "I thought you and Jens Kubek used to be the best of friends."

The comment caught Mark by surprise. "So did I, sir."

"What happened?"

"I'm not sure. He was different when I came back from San Francisco. Then last summer, when I was reinstated into the brass band, he wasn't any too pleased."

"I see." Mr. Schoggen adjusted his thick glasses.

"Jens seems unhappy a lot of the time. I think it's because his papa gets onto him so much. Sometimes right in front of the customers. It's awfully embarrassing." Mark hadn't really thought about this too much and was surprised at what he heard himself saying. "And Dirk, his older brother, is hard on him as well. The brother who was kind to him died of influenza."

Mr. Schoggen nodded. "I've been in the shop on occasions, myself. I believe you see the situation correctly. Everyone needs encouragement from someone." He shuffled around a few sheets of music on his desk, then said, "I tell you what. I'm going to have a talk with Jens, but if he doesn't listen, there's not much I can do. He has to make correct decisions on his own."

"Yes, sir." Mark wasn't sure why a teacher would be telling him these things.

"I do want to ask one thing of you."

"What is it?"

"If you can find a way—any way—to show Jens that you still want to be his friend, I encourage you to do so. He needs you, Mark."

Mark was at a loss. What could he ever do to show Jens what he was feeling in his heart? It seemed impossible. "I'll try, sir."

"You'll not be sorry."

As Mark walked home alone that day, he thought of a plan. It would take some precise timing, but he felt sure he could do it.

Chapter 15
The Christmas List

That evening in his room, Mark practiced so he could write in two different styles, both different from his usual writing. Then he wrote two notes. The first note was to Harvey and signed from Camille. It told Harvey that she truly cared about him more than she did any other boy.

The second note was to Camille. Mark signed it from Harvey. This note told Camille that Harvey thought she was the most beautiful girl in the world. As he wrote it, Mark realized he was ending any chance of ever having Camille to himself.

When he was finished, Mark took the note signed from Camille into the bathroom and sprinkled a few drops from Mama's bottle of rose water on the paper. Now for the next step in his plan.

During band hour each day, students were either in the auditorium for choir practice or in the library study hall. It was the only time all day when the eighth-grade classroom was completely empty.

Mark waited for a day when he could slip upstairs to the classroom during band and put the notes in the right desks without being seen. Finally a bad cold gave him the perfect excuse. Because of his runny nose, Mark asked Mr. Schoggen if he could go to the room and fetch a clean handkerchief from his desk.

Miss Gallaway was on duty in study hall, so Mark knew the classroom would be empty. It took only a few minutes to enter the room, place the correct letters in the correct desks, grab his handkerchief, and return to the band room. Now he would wait to see what happened.

Carol announced to the family that she wanted to cook Thanksgiving dinner and have everyone come to her new home for the meal. She convinced Mama to take a break from all the cooking for one year.

But in the weeks leading up to the holiday, Mama and Stella were cooking anyway. "Just a few things to take along and help out," Mama told the family.

Before Thanksgiving arrived, Harvey and Camille were making eyes at one another from across the classroom. Harvey began carrying Camille's books home from school, and Jens looked more glum than Mark had ever seen him. It made Mark almost sick with guilt. Perhaps he shouldn't have meddled. During that same week, Harvey and Jens were both expelled from band.

Having Thanksgiving dinner in a new place seemed odd, but even Uncle Abe and Aunt Elise agreed that change was good for all of them. Carol pulled off her first sit-down company dinner with ease. Her kitchen help was superb, and the food was delicious. Carol beamed as the compliments flew freely about the table, and she looked happier than Mark had ever seen her.

Peter and Louise were there, and Louise was wearing an opal engagement ring. The thought made Mark heave a sigh. Before you knew it, there'd be yet another wedding in the family.

During dinner, Christopher announced that when the automobile dealer opened his doors in January, he planned to purchase an automobile. "Sort of a family Christmas gift," he told the group.

Holly nearly jumped out of her chair. "You mean it, Christopher? We'll have our own automobile parked right outside our house?"

"We sure will."

"Yippee!" she squealed.

"Holly Morgan," Mama said firmly, "mind your manners."

"Well, now, Polly," Uncle Abe said, "it is something to squeal about. That's great news, Chris. Why, before long, everyone will be driving automobiles, and the buggies and wagons will be a thing of the past."

"Do you really think so?" Mama asked. Mark could hear the doubt in her voice.

"He's right," Edward agreed. "And it's coming faster than any of us realize."

Mark, too, was quite pleased. He was sure Christopher would let him drive often. But somewhere in the back of his mind, he kept thinking about Jens.

That evening when they returned home, Christopher called his family into the parlor. When they were all settled, he thanked them for being so patient through the long process of writing his first novel. "I know it's been difficult, but you've all helped me so much."

"All we did was stay out of your way," Holly said in a not-very-nice tone.

"Holly," Mama chided.

"Oh, she's right, Polly. It's true. But now that the second novel is underway, and since the money situation is easier, I want each of you to write down what you'd like for Christmas and give it to me in the next few days. I'd like to get each of you something special."

"But Christopher, you said the automobile would be our family gift."

"That's true, Polly. But I want to do something for each of you personally as well."

"Thank you, Christopher," Allyson said, "that's thoughtful of you."

As Holly and Mark were going upstairs later, Mark said, "Do you know what you'll ask for?"

She shook her head. "No, do you?"

"Why not come into my room and let's compare."

Holly's face lit up. "That's a good idea."

As Mark followed her up the stairs, he realized he'd spent hardly any time with his sister in the past few months. Perhaps she was feeling as lonely as he was.

Within moments, she was in his room dressed in her wrapper with her long hair hanging about her shoulders. She had a pad of paper and a pencil. "I was thinking about a new party dress. I haven't had a really nice new dress in ever so long—except for the one for Carol's wedding. What do you think?"

Mark sat down beside her on the bed. "I think we should ask Christopher for something that doesn't require money."

"What do you mean?"

"Hand me the paper and pencil." On the pad he began to write a list. Holly moved closer to look over his shoulder and read as he wrote:

> *We, the undersigned, would like to ask for the*
> *following for Christmas:*
> *A father who will talk to us, play games with us,*
> *read Scripture with us, pray with us, go to church*
> *with us, and listen to us. It doesn't cost much, but it*
> *would be worth a million dollars.*
>
> *Your loving children,*
> *Holly and Mark*

Holly's eyes shone with tears and happiness. "What a wonderful, wonderful thing to ask," she said softly.

"You're in agreement?"

"Complete agreement. Let me sign!"

After they'd folded the note and placed it in an envelope, Mark said, "Holly, I've buried myself in my music and in my own problems this past year. I've not been much of a brother because of that. I apologize. I want you to know if you ever want to talk, I'll listen."

"Oh, Mark." Holly threw her arms around his neck and wept. Mark wasn't sure what to do, so he just softly patted her back. "Thank you," she said with a sniffle.

"Do you want to talk now?" he asked.

She let go of his neck, and he got her a handkerchief from his bureau drawer. "Mark," she said dabbing at her eyes, "do you think I'm a bad girl?"

Mark thought about the grief his sister had caused Mama ever since last summer. He wasn't sure how to answer. "Misled perhaps," he said, "but not bad."

"Did you know that all the girls in my class are jealous because I'm friends with Camille? And all of them are furious because of it."

"Are you sure it's jealousy?"

"Of course. None of them have friends who are in eighth grade—only me. What else could it be but jealousy?"

"Perhaps they don't like the way you act when you're around Camille."

"I don't act any differently when I'm with Camille." She paused. "Do I?"

"Only you can answer that. But you need to ask yourself if friendship with a girl like Camille is worth the friendship of all the other girls in your class."

"I thought it was."

"And now?"

"Now I'm not too sure. But I'll think it over."

"Let me know."

"I will. Thanks, Mark." She stepped toward the door. "Good night."

"Good night, Holly."

Pulling his journal out of his desk, Mark began to write:

Dear Michael,
*   I think I've learned what's been troubling Holly. . . .*

The next morning at breakfast, Holly seemed more like her

old self. On the table next to Christopher's plate were the notes he'd asked for. He smiled and tucked them into the inside pocket of his suit jacket.

As Mark and Holly started out for school, the morning was bitter cold with low-hanging clouds. There would probably be snow on the ground before the day was out. In spite of the grayness, the teachers sent the students outside to play at recess. Holly's excitement about their new family automobile was spilling over. She'd told just about everybody.

Just as Mark suspected, the news rubbed Jens the wrong way. He came walking up to Mark and said, "Well, now you'll really be the hotshot of the neighborhood, won't you? Just what you need, Mark Morgan, something else to show off about. As if you don't have enough already."

"Don't talk that way, Jens," Mark said. "*I'm* not buying the automobile—"

"I suppose you'll be driving to school every day with your nose in the air." Jens stepped toward Mark, gave him a shove, and said in a loud voice, "Show-off!"

Mark staggered to keep his balance, but Jens shoved him again. "Stop that, Jens!" he demanded.

"Make me, you big show-off!" Another shove—harder this time. This time, Mark pushed back. That was exactly what Jens was waiting for. In a flash he'd jumped on Mark.

Mark felt the air go out of him as he hit the cold, hard ground. Jens got in one hard punch to Mark's jaw before Mark regained his senses and was able to muster his strength. Jens was tall, but he was also skinny. With one well-aimed push, Mark heaved the lightweight from on top of him, held him in a roll, and quickly had him pinned down to the ground.

Between gasps for air, Mark said, "Jens Kubek, all I want is to be your friend. Now stop fighting me!"

With that, he jumped up and let Jens go. By now they were surrounded by a tight cluster of onlookers. Jens scrambled to his feet and limped off through the knot of kids without saying a word.

Mark rubbed his aching jaw. He thought what Mr. Schoggen had said about trying to be Jens's friend. It sure looked like an impossible mission.

CHAPTER 16
The Notes

Mark and Jens had to stay after school for fighting on the playground. Miss Gallaway scolded them soundly. Then she said, "I can remember when you two were the best of friends. Now look at you, fighting like two alley cats. Shame on you."

Neither of them said a word. Although Mark knew he'd done nothing wrong, Miss Gallaway made them apologize and shake hands. Mark could tell Jens didn't want to, but he didn't have much choice. Jens mumbled his apology and gave a fast handshake without so much as looking Mark in the eyes.

Miss Gallaway didn't bother to mask her disappointment. "That's all, Jens. You may go. Mark, stay here for a few more minutes."

"Yes, ma'am." Mark watched Jens hurry to the cloakroom to grab his things.

Miss Gallaway walked to the blackboards and erased them. After a few moments, she said, "Jens has seemed terribly unhappy lately. Do you know why, Mark?"

"No, ma'am."

"At one time you were his friend. And I thought at one time Camille was his friend, too. Now even Harvey has turned away from him."

Mark swallowed hard.

"Do you know anything about all this, Mark?"

"Why should I?"

Miss Gallaway came back to her desk and sat down. She looked squarely at Mark. "I'll ask it a different way. Do you want to tell me what you know about the situation?"

Mark's guilty conscience gnawed at his insides, just as it had been ever since he'd planted the notes. "I do know a little bit."

"Perhaps you'd like to tell me that little bit."

"I know it was wrong. I should never have interfered."

"*You* interfered? Tell me how."

Mark blurted out the whole thing—how he wrote the notes and planted them in the desks. "I thought if Harvey and Camille started liking one another maybe Jens and I could become friends again. Harvey and Camille are the ones who've caused all the problems."

"And now how do you feel?"

"Terrible," Mark confessed. "I never knew it would make Jens so sad."

Miss Gallaway opened the drawer of her desk, pulled out two pieces of paper, and handed them to him.

Mark gasped. "Miss Gallaway! These are the notes!"

She smiled. "I know. I happened to be in the hallway that day. I saw you come into the room, and I wondered why it was taking you so long. I peeked in and saw you planting the notes."

"Oh my." Mark's knees felt all rubbery. "Then these notes didn't. . ."

"No. The notes had nothing to do with Harvey liking Camille. A teacher sees many things, Mark. I saw the looks between Harvey and Camille, so I decided to wait and let you stew for a time. At least now you can see the damage the notes *might* have caused."

"Oh yes, ma'am. I do see, and I'm so sorry." Mark suddenly felt an awful weight lift from his shoulders.

"Jens needs you right now," their teacher went on, "but as long as you thought you were the cause of his grief, your guilt kept you from reaching out to him."

Mark nodded. What she said made sense. He held up the notes. "Do you want these back?"

"You wrote untrue words there, Mark. Untrue words that you thought you'd never be able to recover. What would you like to do with them?"

"I'd like to tear them in tiny pieces and drop them in the trash can."

Miss Gallaway smiled. "Be my guest."

It had been lightly snowing all afternoon, and as Mark started home, the snow was coming down thick and steady. In spite of his heavy coat, woolen muffler, and his cap with the lined ear-flaps, he was chilled to the bone. A welcome rush of warm air and the aroma of hot chocolate greeted him as he opened the front door.

From down the hall, he heard Stella say, "Is that you, Mark?"

"Yes, ma'am."

"There's a letter for you on the hall table."

"Thank you." Hopefully it was a letter from Peter. He wrote so seldom these days. And Peter's last note to Mama let them know he was going to Louise's home in Duluth for Christmas. Mark shook off the wetness from his coat, hung up his things, and went to the hall table.

He stared down at the letter on top of the mail. It couldn't be! But there it was. He reached out and touched the name on the corner of the envelope, *John Philip Sousa, Esq.* Slowly Mark picked up the envelope. Using the letter opener, he slit the envelope open. His hand was trembling.

Dear Mark,

Thank you for your letter, which caught up with me in Buffalo. You sound like an intelligent lad with wise questions. I will be coming to Minneapolis next week for a meeting of authors, artists, and composers. I want to meet privately with you when I come and answer your questions. That is, with permission of your stepfather, the up-and-coming novelist Christopher Wilkins.

Until then, I remain very truly yours,
John Philip Sousa

Mark let out a whoop and jumped into the air. When he hit the floor, he was racing down the hall to Christopher's office and banging on the door. When a grinning Christopher surprised

Mark by opening the door, Mark nearly fell inside.

"Yes? Do I hear an excited voice out here?"

Mark waved the letter. "It's from. . .He wants to. . .I mean, can we. . ."

Christopher reached out and put his arm around Mark's shoulder. "Mr. Sousa and I have talked on the telephone, Mark. We've set up the meeting here at our home on the Saturday afternoon following the forum at the hotel."

"Can Jens come, too? He and I both need to hear this. Can he, please?"

Christopher laughed. "Of course, Jens can come, but please don't invite the rest of your class."

"Oh no, I wouldn't do that." Mark's heart was pounding in his throat. This was an unbelievable turn of events. "Thank you, Christopher. Thanks so much." Mark realized then that Christopher's strong arm was wrapped around him. Mark turned and gave his stepfather a hug. "You're great!"

"But I didn't do anything."

"Oh yes, you did," Mark replied. "If you weren't an author, this never could have happened." Mark remembered how he'd hated all the long hours Christopher had spent in his office last summer. But now. . . Mark stepped back toward the door. "I'm going to Jens's house to tell him."

"It's snowing. Why don't you use the telephone?"

Mark waved the letter over his head as he went down the hall. "You can't see a letter like this over the telephone lines!"

In a few minutes, Mark was once again bundled up and back out in the cold snow. This time, he didn't care about the wetness, the thick snow, or the cold wind. Mr. and Mrs. Kubek probably thought he was daft when he came barreling into the butcher shop. "Where's Jens? I've gotta see Jens. This is important."

"He's upstairs sulking," Mr. Kubek said. "A sulky lad he's become lately."

"He won't be sulky after this," Mark declared as he bounded up the stairs two at a time. Pounding on the door, he called out to Jens to open up.

"Go away," came Jens's voice from the other side. "I don't want to see you."

Mark opened the door anyway. Jens sat doing his arithmetic homework at the kitchen table. "You *want* to see me, Jens Kubek," Mark said. "Wait'll you see this."

Mark sat down beside Jens and placed the letter right under his nose.

Jens studied it a minute, then looked at Mark. "This isn't really from him, is it?"

"Open it and see."

Jens pulled out the letter and read it. "You're going to meet him in person?"

"We're going to meet him in person. You and I, Jens. Together."

Jens sat there a moment, then he sniffed and wiped his cheek with the back of his hand. "Thanks, Mark. Thanks a lot."

"Hey, what are friends for? You've probably got a lot more pictures of him than I do. You're his biggest fan!"

"Mark," Jens said, pulling out his handkerchief to blow his nose, "are you going to your uncle's to practice this evening?"

Mark nodded. "I go every day, without fail."

"Could I? I mean, do you think he'd care if there were two of us practicing in the carriage house? I may not be in band, but I'd like to keep on practicing."

"Uncle Abe care? Of course not. Get your coat and horn and let's go. Wrap up well, Jens. It's mighty cold out there."

132

CHAPTER 17
John Philip Sousa

Stella served tea in the parlor using Mama's best silver, which was used only for special occasions. Mark and Jens had brought in plenty of wood to make sure the fire was roaring in the parlor fireplace. Now Mr. Sousa was seated comfortably in the overstuffed chair. Christopher sat in the chair opposite him, and Jens and Mark were on the floor near the warm hearth.

Mr. Sousa was dressed in a casual tweed coat with pants that didn't really match. His beard, which was dark in all the photographs, was actually streaked with gray. With no military hat on his head, it was obvious that his hair was thinning.

There were no brass buttons today, no pomp or pageantry. Just a guest in their parlor quietly visiting with them and answering their questions. Although Mark had been nervous as a cat all day, the moment Mr. Sousa walked in, Mark was at ease. A gentle man, Mr. Sousa had kind eyes.

Mr. Sousa wanted to know all about their participation in the brass band. They told him everything—Jens even admitted that he'd been dropped from the band.

"I could tell by your letter that you've been confused by the different types of music going around today," Mr. Sousa said. "But there's no need for confusion. Music in and of itself is neither good nor bad, but there can be very bad performances of very good music. Why some ragtime music is so bad it makes you want to bite your grandmother."

The comment made them all chuckle.

"But in the Sousa band," he continued, "we play everything to perfection. It's the treatment rather than the type of music that's vital." Mr. Sousa sipped his hot tea and stared at the leaping flames. "We can play a common street melody with just as much care as if it were the best thing ever put on a program. I have washed its face, put a clean dress on it, put a frill around its neck, and pretty stockings. It is now an attractive thing, entirely different from the frowzy-headed thing of the gutter."

Mark and Jens looked at one another. Mark grinned because Jens's eyes were shining!

"Mr. Klawinski and your school conductor," Mr. Sousa said, "want you boys to learn to follow them, to be the best participants of the group that you can possibly be. That's important. While I have many virtuosos in my band, still and yet, when they play with the group, it sounds as though it were all one in tone and harmony."

Mark knew that was true from when he'd heard the Sousa band in concert.

"But aside from all that," Mr. Sousa continued, "the most important issue here is obedience and respect for your parents." Mr. Sousa's gentle but piercing brown eyes were now fixed on Mark. "I believe you mentioned that your mother did not approve of ragtime music. Is that correct?"

"Yes, sir."

"Then you should obey her first and foremost." He smiled and smoothed his thick beard. "If you do well in obeying your parents, you will have no trouble obeying your band director—no matter who that director is."

They talked of many things that afternoon, but mostly about music. It was a day Mark knew he would remember forever. He took careful notice of every detail so he could record it in his journal that evening.

The visit was over much too quickly. An automobile arrived to take the March King to the train station. They followed him out into the hall, where he pulled on his great overcoat. Reaching into his pocket, he said, "Here boys. Because of your desire to better yourselves and your music, I'd like to give you a little gift."

With that Mr. Sousa pulled out a pair of his famous white kid gloves. He handed one to Mark and one to Jens. Mark looked at the glove in disbelief. It was slightly soiled and soft as a piece of pure silk.

"Perhaps one day I'll meet you again," Mr. Sousa said. "Perhaps you'll be playing in a band somewhere, or perhaps you'll be auditioning for me. Until then, may God bless."

"Thank you, sir," Mark whispered, his voice croaking. "Thank you very much."

Jens echoed his thanks as they shook the man's hand and

he stepped out the door into another blowing snowstorm.

"We're all going to the benefit concert," Christopher announced at supper one evening. Christmas was just around the corner.

"What's that supposed to mean?" Mama asked, eyeing Christopher suspiciously.

"It means we're all going."

"But Christopher," Allyson put in, "you've never gone to the mission before. In all the time that Mama's been helping Aunt Elise, you've never gone."

Christopher gave a sheepish smile. "I know, but that's all changing. We're renting a carriage from the livery, and we're going as a family."

Holly glanced at Mark and winked. He knew what she was thinking. Their Christmas list had worked.

"Might I ask what prompted this?" Mama asked. "Not that I'm ungrateful, mind you."

"You should know, my dear," Christopher said.

"Was it my request for my Christmas gift?" Mama asked, smiling.

"Indeed it was, Polly. And Allyson's, and Mark's and Holly's as well."

Mama looked around at her three children. "Why, Christopher, what do you mean?"

"I would have to be a pretty stiff-necked fellow not to have gotten your point. I suppose you all put your heads together to do this to me."

"Put our heads together?" Holly said. "What're you talking about?"

"Don't act like you don't know," Christopher said. "You can confess now."

"Mark and I wrote our list together," Holly confessed, "but that's all."

Allyson laughed. "I asked Christopher to give us more of himself for Christmas. Mama, is that what you asked for as well?"

Mama was shaking with laughter. "It is. Well, Mr. Wilkins, what do you think of that?"

"I think the Lord is speaking to me to be a more attentive husband and father!" He pushed his plate away and stood up. "If you'll all meet me in the parlor, we'll have Stella bring dessert to us there. We're going to have family worship time this evening. The first of many."

"Yippee!" Holly shouted as she jumped up out of her chair.

"Holly, please," Mama said. "Mind your manners."

"It's all right, Polly." Christopher put his arm around Mama's shoulders as they walked toward the parlor. "She has every reason to be happy."

Prior to the benefit concert, Mark was to meet with the band members in the rehearsal hall. His family would be going to the mission separately. Following a brief rehearsal, the band members rode to the mission in an omnibus.

The mission was crowded. Mark was up on stage and in position for the first number before he managed to find his family. To his surprise, Jens was sitting with them. Mark wanted to wave, but that would be breaking all rules. All he could do was smile. He wondered if inviting Jens had been Christopher's idea. What a great stepfather he had!

Holly and Maureen were seated next to each other and were whispering and laughing. Maureen had let him know a week or so ago that she and Holly were good friends again.

Aunt Elise, Uncle Abe, and Maureen had been at the mission

all day helping with decorations and refreshments. The mission itself was much different than Mark had expected. It was large and clean. The children had been brought in from the orphanage down the street and were seated in the front rows. Sitting on the end of the first row, a wide-eyed little boy who looked to be about six or seven stared at Mark through the entire concert. At one point Mark winked at him, and the boy's somber face broke into a grin.

The program went off without a hitch. Aunt Elise addressed the crowd. She described the work of the rescue mission and the orphanage and explained how businessmen could help. She then introduced several men whose lives were turned around because of the ministry of the mission.

Mark was amazed as he listened to these men tell how they'd been skid-row bums before being helped by the mission. He was ashamed that he'd resented the time Mama spent here as a volunteer. After all, she helped out only three afternoons a week. Surely he could share her for three afternoons!

The brass band was given a standing ovation and played three encores. Following the concert, refreshments were served in the kitchen area. As Mark stepped down from the stage and maneuvered through the crowd, he felt a tug at his coat. It was the wide-eyed little boy.

"Mister," he said, "may I touch your shiny buttons? May I?"

Mark smiled. The little boy had called him mister. He probably seemed like one of the men to this little guy. "Of course," Mark said. He reached down and lifted the boy up onto the steps that led to the stage. The child was light as a feather. "You can touch the braid, too, if you want."

The boy's brown eyes grew wider as he ran his finger along the braid on the sleeve cuff, then touched the brass buttons.

"What's your name?" Mark asked.

"Charles."

"Well, Charles. Let's go get something to eat."

Charles shook his head. "I have to stay with my group."

"Then let's get you back to your group, and I'll see you later in the kitchen."

After dropping off Charles, Mark pushed through the crowd to his family. As he did, people patted him on the back and shook his hand, showering him with praise and compliments. Mark felt about ten feet tall. Even Jens told him how great the band had sounded.

"Next summer," Jens said, "I'll be back in my uniform again. And this time I won't mess things up. I know better now!"

Later, Aunt Elise came up to Mark and Jens, who were standing eating cake and drinking punch. "There you are, boys," she said. "I've been looking everywhere for you."

Mark swallowed his mouthful of sweet cake before answering, "Do you need us to do something for you?"

Aunt Elise smiled. "In a manner of speaking. See that businessman over there?" She pointed to a corner of the room.

Mark nodded. "That's Mr. Beasom, owner of Beasom's Music Store downtown."

"That's right. He just told me his heart has been touched this evening. He wants to donate a few band instruments to the orphanage. I was wondering if you two boys would consider coming over on Saturday afternoons to help these children learn the basics of music."

Mark thought of the little boy named Charles. He glanced over at Jens. "What do you think, Jens?"

"I'd have to ask Mama and Papa, but I'd very much like to help." He gave Mark a nudge in the ribs. "We may not know as much about music as Mr. Klawinski. . ."

"Or Mr. Sousa," Mark chimed in.

"Or Mr. Sousa," Jens repeated, "but we could teach the children what we do know."

Aunt Elise nodded. "It's settled then. I'll get back to you with the details later. Our orphanage teachers are going to be thrilled."

Jens took another big bite of cake. With his mouth full, he said, "Doesn't that beat all, Mark? Five months ago I was kicked out of a band, two months ago I was kicked out of another, and now I'm a music teacher!"

They laughed together at the wonder of it all.

CHAPTER 18

Friends

On the day before school was to let out for the Christmas holiday, Mark went with Jens to talk to Mr. Schoggen. After they had agreed to help out at the orphanage, Mark suggested to Jens that he talk with the band director. At first Jens was totally against the idea. "He'll never want me back," he protested.

"I'll go with you," Mark told him. "Just give Mr. Schoggen a chance."

It took all Mark's powers of persuasion to get the reluctant Jens into the band room during their lunch hour. After a long discussion, and after Jens explained to Mr. Schoggen that he was now very serious about doing his best and how he was practicing with Mark at his uncle Abe's, the kindly instructor reinstated Jens into Fair Oaks Elementary School Band.

When they came out of the band room, Mark slung his arm across Jens's shoulder. "Together again," he said.

Jens slung his arm around Mark's shoulder. "Together again," he echoed. As they walked arm-in-arm, they happened to see Camille and Harvey walking up the stairs ahead of them at the far end of the hallway.

"Did you ever notice," Jens said softly, "that Camille Wilmot has a very loud giggle?"

"A very loud giggle," Mark said.

"Somewhat annoying, wouldn't you agree?"

"I agree wholeheartedly."

Jens snickered. "Not nearly as beautiful as a clear note from my clarinet."

"Or a clear note from my trumpet."

They laughed together as they headed up the stairs to their classroom.

"You know what, Jens?"

"What, Mark?"

"You're going to be one of the first ones to ride in our new automobile. I may even teach you to drive myself—that is, if Christopher agrees."

"Thanks, Mark, old pal."

"Don't mention it, Jens, old pal."

As Mark and Jens entered the classroom talking and laughing together, Miss Gallaway put her finger to her mouth. "Boys! Please! The holiday hasn't started yet. School is still in session."

But their teacher was smiling.

There's More!

The American Adventure continues! In *Clash with the Newsboys,* Lydia and Carl Schmidt, Holly and Mark's cousins, are in danger. Their father is a union officer, and someone who doesn't like his work leaves threatening messages at their home. When Carl reads about some union families who are killed in Colorado, he worries that the same thing might happen to his family.

Then Germany invades Belgium and starts a war in Europe. Lydia and Carl are harassed at school for their German background. Just when they think things can't get worse, they learn that the newsboys they have befriended are threatening to attack the newspaper offices. Will Lydia and Carl be able to stop the newsboys in time? And what can they do to keep their family safe?

You're in for the ultimate
American Adventure!
Collect all 48 books!